The Chief's Court

The Chief's Court

Johnson Kobia Juma Impwi

EXCELLER BOOKS™
A GLOBAL PRESS

The Chief's Court

Cover design by Exceller Books using resources from Pixabay.com

ISBN: 978-93-93734-09-9

First published in India in 2022 by Exceller Books

Address: G1, Dream Apartment, Degree College Road, Belgharia, Kolkata, 700056, India

EXCELLER BOOKS™
A GLOBAL PRESS

www.excellerbooks.com

Dedication

"I dedicate this book to my parents: John M'Impwi M'Tuerandu and Joanina Ciakalaine M'Impwi, who learnt and appreciated the power and authority of the colonial government agents as prison wander and a subject in the 1940s and 1950s and had experienced the colonial supremacy and power before and after my birth in late 1956 respectively. The colonial policies taught them and became an eye opener to them, and they took me to school to acquire the Whiteman's education and skills. This book is dedicated to them today, tomorrow, and forever."

Table of Contents

The Traditional doctor
wears pride on his paraphernalia bag.

Johnson Kobia Juma Impwi

Chapter One

"We are here in the Chief's Court. We are here to hear our relative's case before the chief's elders. We must listen and give our side of the story before the elders arbitrate. The elders must hear the two parties before they conclude the case," said Mr. Adhamu to his friend Mindame. There were many people in the Chief's Court; there were elderly people, both men and women, and a few youths. They sat in a circle kin to *mulami,* the Ndemaru cultural house of elders around the compound, while others just stood. Those who stood had not carried their *Omulua,* the three-legged stool that each elder attending a case in the chief's court had to carry, knowing very well that a chief's court was not a place to go and leave in a hurry. Therefore, whoever came to the chief's court, had always to be prepared to sit and listen or talk when allowed until the sun sank down the hills or a case was settled with finality.

The chief's elders were already present, but the parties had been overheard saying that the chair of the court, Mr. Kindiana, had not yet arrived. However, it would not take long for him to arrive. Mr. Kindiana was known to arrive a few minutes before the chief stepped out of his aboard. "I did not want to arrive early to discuss the case. I did not want to have preconceived judgement through some winks or blinks of some cheeky party member," Mr. Kindiana would give his excuse for lateness. Once he arrived and settled, the court could begin.

Some people in the compound were having secret sessions with the chief's elders. Murmurs and 'snorting' of noses kin to that of a snuffer makes when the snuff is 'hot' were heard repeatedly. There were a few individuals who always behaved like the power brokers of today who would disappear through the thickets around the *mulami* momentarily, only to reappear later.

Their behaviour was rebuked by the chief, but they would defend themselves by saying they had gone aside to cut the saliva.

After some time, Mr. Kindiana arrived, and things seemed to settle, ready for the case to start. However, many attendants were seemingly unsettled. Cases were many, and murmurs began flying around, cautioning the possibility of punishment to those who seemed to undermine the chief's court from their queer behaviour. The parties that had cases sat or stood in small groups. They were either rehearsing their presentation or choosing who would speak on behalf of the group. Clearly, it seemed even in the chief's court, lobbying was inevitable. By this time, more people had arrived, and quite a sizeable crowd was present.

The chief's compound was almost full of those who had come to present their cases and others who had come to defend themselves or listen to arbitration. Some witnesses had come to say what they had witnessed. However, some could have been masqueraders who had come to tamper with truth in their witnessing. Inside the Chief's Court, there were elders of different ages. They all conversed with the traditional culture of Amakia and the Amakia council of elders in the unwritten constitution.

Each party in the case needed well-versed advocates, who had to be members of the Amakia council of elders. They would discuss the laws and constitution of Amakia, while non-members of Amakia would come to listen or to witness. The group members held the first stage in the administration of justice in the court. All clans and villages were represented in the court. The Chief never left any subjects to imagine being discriminated against or not represented in such serious cases.

All the cases in the Chief's Court required professional handling by elders versed with the traditions. They needed elders who had reached the pinnacle of the wisdom of the chief's court rulings and mastered the cultural and oral constitution. There were cases of debt payment, debt breaches, land acquisition, land payments especially using livestock as the means of exchange, land ownership by individuals and the clans, payment or non-payment of dowry, physical injury of a person or animals, breach of agreement, especially on payments, cheating, denying with other people's property, divorce, biological ownership of children, claims of animals among others.

When the Chief stood up, everyone stood up and bowed. This was a sign that the session had started. Then, Mr. Kindiana took his position at his usual position. It was a sign that the cases had started officially. Throats were cleared, and three-legged stools were firmed as those whose ages were clearly marked by their white hair or wisdom of their spoken word and deeds. "Elders of the chief's court, the *Amakia council of elders* representatives, different ages and *agesets,* welcome to the court," the Chief welcomed people after clearing his throat.

The elders listened to cases in succession and sometimes with agitated emotions. The procedure started simple but focused. The Chief allowed the plaintiff to present his or her case before the elders. Then the respondent was allowed to dispute the presentation by the plaintiff. Each party was allowed to have an advocate or advocates assisting. The two parties were at liberty to engage any person to be their traditional lawyer. The party was also allowed to engage members of the elders' group to ask questions on the party's side in assistance, especially to enable the elders to understand the issue well.

The elders listened carefully before they took the secret session, and not all people were allowed in the secret session.

This group was composed of those who had graduated as elders and passed the highest level of traditional and cultural education. Usually, very few members reach this level. It was a rigorous process that saw someone reach this level of admittance to the elders' most refined bar. You did not need any criminal or social misbehaviour known to your equals, villagers, women, or even children. The admittance criteria were tight and guarded; being a member of this court's group was an ultimate measure of social-cultural purity. These men handled the tough cases. Others were left behind after the secret session to await the final judgement, which the two parties must abide by. And they must comply with the elders' ruling before judgment was delivered. The elders would appoint one of their own to provide the ruling to the witnessing public. The judgement was then delivered. If one party was dissatisfied with the ruling, they were allowed to appeal through other judges and advocates within the same court or in any other court. Still, they must be within the same community or an area prescribed by the particular members of the Amakia council of elders.

Women were barred from taking the Amakia council of elders' oath. Women who were married and already had children and those who belonged to *Ambenyi, Bukia,* and *Dombiru* age groups among the women were all classified in the same category as children. In most cases, they were abounded by these rules of engagement, with little or almost nothing to do to change the circumstances of their position. This did not mean that children were not well-protected by the group members. On the contrary, they, as well as the widows and other vulnerable minorities, were well-protected and nobody could dare harass them. However, people, who could not meet their obligations, were subjected to public humiliation. Either you got a public bashing, or your songs were composed to castigate you on the paths when women and children were going to get firewood and on water points as boys watered the cattle.

In the whole tribe, it is a big shame for a person to be charged with failing to honour debts. This will be discussed by the members of the group, those advocates who have been paid by the respective party to come and listen, and those who are there as traditional lawyers of neither party.

When Mr. Kindiana opened his mouth and strung the ground with his staff, all the groups went quiet. It was time to start hearings. The sun had begun standing upright on the heads of the people. "Elders of all the groups, the sun does not wait for the wise man to make his judgement," he said after clearing his throat.

Silence fell, and people started moving to the centre. Some parties began complaining about the little time they had been given to consult.

“Mr. Kindiana, we cannot start the case before people are satisfied with consolidating their defences by consulting the wise men from their sides,” Mr. Adamu implored. There was a murmur of appreciation.

"That is very true; all people must be satisfied with the rulings that shall be made here," Mr. Mindame chipped in.

"Once this court makes a ruling, it is binding. We need to let people feel they are actually at the chief's Court," one of the elders made a roaring baritone statement from the crowd. He was called Mr. Mwandandu. Mr. Mwandandu was a truthful man. People listed whenever he made a statement, not because of his thunderous bass voice but because he never lied. It was unheard of for elders to lie in this community. After this murmur and complaints, the people dispersed to their groups. More time was allocated to wrap up the analysis of the cases to be heard before the Chief's court that day.

There were many cases that day. There were cases of debt breaches that needed keen listening and wise judgement. Such cases had very difficult rules to follow during the arbitration. If one party did not honour a debt, the complainant informed the elders when the contract was not honoured. The elders would then investigate and inquire about getting an answer for the 'failed' or aborted payment. They would strive to see who did not honour their part or whether the accusation was genuine or not. If the accusation is genuine, the defaulter is forced to pay. But the court was very lenient and did not attach interest or fines on top of the actual debt. The court's fairness was always hailed and trusted by all the parties having cases of all types. The accused paid only the very debt they owed the other party. The offending party was allowed to commit when they would pay the debt. An elder was assigned to collect the debt, remit it to the owner, and report to the chief's court elders. The collection was then presented to the owner by one of the elders appointed by the council of elders. This was done in the elders' presence to avoid another fallout in the future.

The other cases concerned land ownership. This involved land belonging to individuals or the clan. There were individual against individual disputes and clan against clan disputes. These kinds of cases were not handled by the chief's elders. Still, they were instead listened to by The Amakia elders, who were conversant with the history, law, and constitution of the Amakia council of elders. This group of elders was very few and far apart. Before you joined them, you were to be thorough in all aspects of life and well-trusted in the community.

***

After another hour of deliberation, the Chief called all the elders to attention. Then he quipped with his usual commanding but respectful voice, "Elders of Amakia council, I call upon you to know that, *Ongela Luo Ogembe*," the sun does not wait for the courts man. After saying this, all the groups that had stayed furiously engaged in the analysis of the cases broke out and started sitting in a circle surrounding the chair where the Chief sat. However, from the circle, it was clear that there was a separation of the parties, the complainants occupying the right side of the circle and the plaintiffs on the left. But a stranger could not tell if there was this demarcation. After the cases opened up under the leadership of Mr. Kindiana, all the people went dead silent. The ants hissed as they collected their meals and disappeared into the thin holes.

One of the senior elders in the court, Mr. Shalu, was a judge in the community and was reputed for his knowledge and wisdom as an elder. In many cases, he had listened to and arbitrated in the community and the clan. He could rarely be found at home because many people with such cases came to hire him as an advocate. He travelled to many places in the community to assist people in solving land problems, proving to be the most complex cases. Also, there was Mr. Shalu, who came from Mutendia clan in the Abika sub-tribe. He listened to a case between two neighbours on a land dispute. Some elders from the community had come both as witnesses and as villains. In such cases, you will not miss a group of elders who either come to collect information to use it to build their daily tidbits on the logs that they sat while playing ajua or use the information to pass the time as they drink the traditional brew, *alingwa*, in the villages.

More often than not, in some instances, during such cases, the elders from different sections of the community visited Karima shrines to pour libation and seek good luck to win such cases.

But the case that was being tackled that day was unique and difficult. I was attended by people of all ages, between fifty and eighty. The numbers already created a sense of urgency and an atmosphere of seriousness to the whole case.

"Where is Nzemba Kadinga?" asked Nzemba Wame, who was invited by the plaintiff, Mr. Alône. He had been invited to listen to his case, but most importantly, to make a presentation before the elders as an experienced Amakia 'council of elders' member. So he conversed with the law and constitution of the Amakia council of elders. Nzemba Wame paced around the seated group of elders, straining his eyes in all directions but without a trace of Nzemba Kadinga. He tried to look for him everywhere but could not find him. By this time, Mr. Kindiana, Mr. Adhamu, and Mr. Mindame started showing restlessness. They had become impatient since every sign showed something was being cooked by some group members. The Chief was vexed by the state of affairs. He was looking fed up too. He held his flywhisk and threw it left to right like one chasing away some invisible mosquitoes. Sometimes he did this whenever he became angry. "Mhhhh..." the Chief coughed. Everybody kept quiet and looked at him. He stamped the ground with his foot. Then he looked far beyond the trees as if consulting his forefathers to get the wisdom to deal with the prevailing situations.

As everybody watched and kept quiet, waiting for the Chief to say something, Nzemba Wame went to a distance and beckoned to one of his colleagues seated among the crowd. Nzemba Kalime approached the spot where Mr. Wame had summoned him. He greeted him with Amakia council of elders' greetings, and Mr. Wame responded similarly. He inquired whether he had met his friend Kadinga who was also to assist him in defending the case in the Amakia court. Mr. Kalime told him that he had not seen him since the last time they had assembled at the same venue a week earlier.

Meanwhile, Mr. Adhamu, Mr. Kindiana, and Mr. Mindame looked at one another in awe. It seemed they had also sensed that a game was being played. After a few looks with the crowd fidgeting, it had become uncomfortable with the queer behaviour of Mr. Wame and Mr. Kalime. Mr. Mwandandu made his thunderous noise to attention again, "*alime ati nakuru mbee.*" "Did we come to spend the night here, elders?" When he asked this question, Mr. Wame and Mr. Kalime stepped a few rocks away (there were rocks placed around for elders who did not carry Omulua to sit on), sat down on a nearby raised ground, and started conversing in low tones. The elders stared at them in disbelief!

Chapter Two

The crowd at the Chief's Court remained mum. But the issues they had come to address were weighty. The Chief's Court was silent but expectant. No one knew who would win and who would lose. All the parties, both the plaintiff and defendants, were confident they would win. There were young and old people, most of whom had come to either support someone or defend themselves. Land was a sensitive issue among the people. It was important because it was the source of food and source of wealth for people. It was on that land where people grew food for their livelihood and also kept livestock for milk and meat, and got blood as food from animals to live on. Cattle and other livestock were also used for bride price. In other words, land supported life in full. So, no one wanted to joke about land-related matters or cases.

There were almost fifty people, mostly elders, in that compound. The quorum had already been realised, and all the parties and the elders were present. The land case was about to begin. Trunks of trees served as seats in that compound, and the presiding judges were seated among the circular seats among other people but could be recognised by the staff they were holding and their advanced ages. Other elders were not judges because they were not initiated into the Amakia council of elders, meaning they were not educated in the laws and constitution of land and land ownership of the clan and community at large.

The chief sat pensively, looking at the crowd. The wrinkles on his face looked like the ridges of an old volcanic mountain. The seriousness of the case ahead of him made him look older than his age. Mr. Kindiana, Mr. Mindame, and Mr. Adamu all sat near him without uttering a word.

After waiting for the orderlies to settle, the chief opened the case. As soon as he stood up to speak, Mr. Kalime and Mr. Wame, who had sat far from the circle of elders discussing matters unknown to the elders, came back running. They knew they would be heavily fined if the chief spoke before they were seated.

“Amakia council of elders of the Chief's court, today we have to dispense with these cases,” the chief spoke.

"I shall not wait for my people to start endless fights over land that our forefathers have shared without problems for many years," he said and coughed a dry cough.

The crowd of elders murmured in unison. They appreciated the efforts brought forward by the chief to remind people of the origins of the land and land use.

A few minutes later, the discussion had started, and the cases had picked momentum. Nzemba Matondu was seen walking into the compound accompanied by three old men holding their official staff and a young man without a staff. When he entered the compound, some elders stood up and met him and his companion. They stood aside and started discussing with him in low tones. Those, who had accompanied him, proceeded to their seats. This act startled everyone so much that even the Chief kept silent for a while. It seemed the Chief's orderlies had been abused.

Five minutes elapsed while Mr. Matondu and his group discussed something in hushed tones. Finally, he joined the other elders who were seated watching Mr. Matondu's group. Before Mr. Matondu sat, he greeted the Amakia council of elders. He then greeted other groups who seemed irritated by his actions. He seemed discriminatory. His greetings were separated in rendition. He knew how to address the groups separately. But without a care, they all responded. Members of the Amakia council of elders responded in their own style of greeting, and the other members responded in the usual and local style. He sat comfortably on one log that was a few feet away from where the Chief sat.

"Mr. Matondu, cases are money and time-consuming, but there is no way we can escape them. Men try to avoid cases, but when they come, we greet them with courage because one cannot run away from them,” a young man commented in clear agitation. Mr. Matondu nodded in agreement but did not comment. He clearly knew the information that was being passed on by the speaker.

There were many opponent judges and advocates seated around Matondu. Matondu's comments could result in implied jurisprudence concerning the case. His silence would not have resulted in anything better, too, since the old *miche* had a way of determining justice. No comments or suggestions, whether real or implied, could result in concaving the justice.

Matondu's brother, Mr. Muili, came, and before he could reach where his brother was seated, he beckoned towards him when he was about twenty meters away. They both retreated to a secluded area about thirty metres away from the people. All the people looked at them. People could see Mr. Muili shaking his head and gesticulating vehemently with his right hand, maybe trying to elaborate a point. In most cases, his brother nodded in approval without saying a word.

The pair put the listeners in a waiting mode. There was a clear show of irritation and hatred, but no one wanted to talk ill for fear of reprisals from the elders.

A few seconds later, Mr. Matondu took his turn and could be seen talking to his brother, but unlike Muili, his actions were not as animated. The duo discussed quietly for a while. After about ten minutes, they returned to the court to join the others. Mr. Matondu had his own real antithesis in one Mr. Kiberi in this case. However, Mr. Kiberi was neither present at the court place nor in the court's compound.

The council elders included Mr. Adhamu, Mr. Mindame, and Kindiana. While the Chief conferred with them, Mr. Kiberi, like a slithering snake, appeared from the court's rear side, which had thicker bushes. He was accompanied by four elderly men, one supporting himself with a stick and had a bald head. All the people looked at them as they sauntered to the court's centre, showing their browning teeth and winding gaps where teeth had already given up living.

"This is one of the senior judges in the Amakia court. Though there are others here, that one is the oldest, considering physical age, talent and experience have a role to play," said Mr. Ndime.

"The presentation also matters," said another elder in agreement.

"We have one Court and one chief," the Chief's calm but firm voice cut in, and everybody kept quiet.

The team, including Mr. Kiberi, got into the compound and sat amid the crowd on the logs that cyclically adorned the grass court. Mr. Kiberi was given a space by a younger man at the foremost log to sit because he was the one to present the case. Most logs had already been occupied by other people who had come earlier. These were not chairs, but logs of trees cut and put down along as chairs in a circular arrangement. The 'advocates' and the 'judges' were also seated in the same circular way. Those, who were parties to the case, went inside the circle to present their issues, and the respondents followed suit. Witnesses, who had something to tell the court, edged closer.

The elders started listening attentively to all the speakers. In the tradition, there was no chairman but elders from various clans and communities who were known to introduce matters. These people are simply referred to as spokespersons, and every home, village, clan, or community had a spokesperson or spokespersons.

One of the spokesmen, appointed by the Chief Mr. Mwandame, stood up and asked the gathering to keep quiet. All the people kept quiet suddenly. The whole ground felt like a grave. People feared contravening the Chief's Court orderlies for fear of reprisals, including fines and outright rebuke. However, there was a slight murmur. The murmuring could not be immediately pointed out to someone but a group of *Nzemba (elder)* and some other complainants who sat on the far left side of the court. After a few minutes of murmuring, the chief stood up and shook his flywhisk. Everybody kept silent.

People feared the wrath of the chief and the possible heavy fines that they would be slapped with in case the Chief got angry and pointed at 'you' as the noise maker. So, whenever he stood up, everybody went dead silent!

The elders requested one of the members, Mr. Miwande, to lead with a word of prayer. All people present stood up except the old man with a bald head. Nzemba Thirina was also willing to stand up. When people understood his intentions as he struggled to stand up, the elders, who were next to him, asked him to remain seated. One of the young men, who was seated behind him, told him silently, “You are our grandfather, remain seated; we shall say your prayers." He held his shoulder to balance him on his three-legged stool. He was shaking, and his knees cracked like dry wood on the fire.

“Thank you, my grandchild; I pray for you to reach my age," Nzemba Thirina said to the young man. All this time, the people, including the chief's elder appointee, Mr. Kwamwi, were looking at the old man as the young man balanced him on his three-legged stool. When Mr. Kwamwi stopped talking, he beckoned Mr. Miwande to say the prayers.

After finishing the prayers, the Chief's appointee introduced the elders from every village and beyond. He also explained to the people why they were there on a Wednesday. Then, he introduced Mzee Thirina and said there was a serious case, which is why they had very old people who had come to attend the case as both an elder and a witness to one party.

Mr. Kwamwi, the chief's appointee, asked the two parties to light a fire. The two parties knew what it means to 'light a fire,' and they were prepared as well. Thus, they went in the direction of the chief's appointee. Mr. Kwamwi pointed towards another elder, Mr. Beka, who was seated a little distance away. Something exchanged hands fast, and then an announcement was made.

"You are cleared, Mr. Matondu," said Mr. Beka. "You can take your seat," he added.

When he was saying all this, the other party, Mr. Kiberi, was searching for his money from the left pocket of his old torn coat. He removed both notes and coins from the pocket and handed the note to Mr. Beka. Then, he handed a polythene paper containing the coins again to Mr. Beka. Mr. Beka, the recipient, initially refused to pick up the money and told Mr. Kiberi to first count the money in his hand in everyone else's presence and then put the money in the polythene paper and hand it over to him.

“I have counted several times before I put them in the polythene paper in my pocket,” said Mr. Kiberi.

“I'm not denying that, but can we count again in my presence for confirmation purposes?” requested Mr. Kwamwi. All this time, everybody was looking at them. Finally, Mr. Kiberi counted the money, which was in the form of coins, and gave it to Mr. Beka for confirmation. The sum was confirmed.

“Thank you, Mr. Kiberi,” said Mr. Beka. The Chief's appointee called other names who had their cases to be listened to on that day. They were six in number. Mr. Beka announced that the parties should be prepared with notes, not coins because coins were wasting a lot of time while counting and confirming the final figure.

Many parties were going around their partners to follow the instructions given by Mr. Beka. Others were a few metres away from the Chief's court within the thickets to exchange coins with notes for the presentation. Everything looked like a barter market: a coin for a note and a note for a coin. After returning from the small secret sessions around the chief's Court and near the very bushes, the last party handed its money to Mr. Beka. The sun had sunk a great deal. It was heading to 4 o'clock in the evening. People, who were in the chief's court, were talking amongst themselves in their respective groups. Others were discussing how they would start the case. Yet others were checking whether their advocates and spokespersons had arrived at the court. At least, the fire had been lit, and the whole court was now alive, with many trying to make statements of knowledge and wisdom about even cases that did not affect them.

"I am losing patience. Time is moving, and cases are not beginning," said Nzemba Thirina. "When are we starting? I'm getting tired of sitting here," he added. Mr. Beka, who was busy counting the money and arranging it in his long pair of trousers' pocket, was not perturbed by such comments. He was going to change the coins into notes. The chief's appointee, Mr. Mwandame, started asking for attention. "Lend me your ears, please. Is there anybody who had his case to be heard today and has not been called?" "Yes," a short-stunted long hairy man shouted. "Can you come forward?" said Mr. Mwandame. The short man in his short trousers came forward. Before he was asked his name, he shouted, "My name is Alibari Wa Kabari, and I come from the Athwe sub-location." People looked at him in surprise because neither the chief's appointee nor anyone else had asked for his name.

Mr. Mwandame consulted his elders, and they did not remember having discussed his case. They neither had seen him before nor had they come across such a name. They all disagreed with him that not only did they not register his case, but they had also never seen him before. After a short discussion, they concluded that he might be a mad man. After a short while, he said, "Somebody has taken my cock from my house; I want a case with him before the chief," the short man shouted again. "Do you want the case with him, or do you report the case to us here?" asked Mr. Mwandame. "I want the case today," responded the short man.

Mr. Mwandame made other elders understand he wanted the case and that he had not registered the case earlier. Mr. Mwandame beckoned Mr. Beka. He told Mr. Beka to listen to the short man and understand his problem. He asked other two elders to interview him well to know where he came from, his assistant chief and chief, and study what he was alleging. They took the man to a secluded place at the corner of the chief's court compound. When they asked him to repeat his name, he did not mistake the name he had shouted a few minutes earlier. When he was asked his name, he said his name was Alibari Wa Kabari from the Urange clan. Since the elders knew the Urange clan, they asked him who his father was.

"My father died a few years ago," he said.

"What was his name?" the elders implored.

"His name was Samu Kakwengo," he answered quickly.

One of the elders, Mr. Tawelo, remembered Makwengo, son of Irwaro.

"Makwengo, son of Irwaro from Urange?" asked Mr. Tawelo.

"That is it," responded Alibari Wa Kabari.

"I have known you, young man; I have even known your mother, Malaku. She comes from our clan, Tabu. Although your father used to address us as in-laws whenever we met, you are now our sister's son, or in other words, you are our nephew. What is your problem, Mr. Alibari Wa Kabari?"

Mr. Alibari Wa Kabari explained his problem and was told to come later if the problem was not very serious. Then, he was asked to go and report to the Urange clan spokesperson, Mr.

Bavule. He was also told to communicate to the chief's court if the clan spokesperson did not solve his problem the way he wanted and if he doubted the ruling of the spokesperson. When he was asked whether he had ever reported the issue to the headman, Mr. Zambila, he admitted that he had not reported it to him. "Go to him and tell him I have sent you," said Mr. Beka. "Thank you, I will communicate to you soon," responded Mr. Alibari wa Kabari.

All this time, the crowd in the chief's Court was silent but visibly irritated by the turn of events. Some of the old men had started getting their tobacco to snuff, while others had started pacing around and cutting the saliva. When the group of men doing the interrogation returned, the sun had already started sinking. Yet no case had been heard fully and determined.

Chapter Three

Mr. Alibari Wa Kabari and the elders interviewing him returned to their positions and sat back. Cases were about to start. The first case was a land case between Mr. Matondu and Mr. Kiberi. The land was in the Sakali clan, an area well-known to the elders in the chief's court. Mr. Matondu had taken the case to the chief's court because Mr. Kiberi claimed that he inherited the land from his father, Bowichu, who had planted yams and had kept livestock in that piece of land before the family migrated to the Urange clan.

Mr. Kiberi, on the other hand, claimed that the land belonged to him through his great, great, great grandfather, Mr. Abendo. The latter had owned the land from his ancestors before the ancestors of Mr. Kwendu settled there together with others from their migratory area of origin in Bugale. He told the elders that he was ready to compromise all the traditional customs to retain his ancestors' land.

He added that he was ready to abide by any traditional law because his father Mbilongo, who had died ten years earlier, had marketed the history of that land to him. "The land is ours through our ancestors who settled here as the first occupants and when it was still virgin land. There were a few wild animals when he settled there. Some animals, which were living there, have since become extinct. Others present today are elephants, buffaloes, and black spotted hyenas, among others," narrated Mr. Kiberi. He told them that his father also told him that, according to his ancestors, they were the first people to rear wild goats and deer, which joined the domestic goats while grazing in the bush.

"There were no such people. There were only wild animals, some of which supplemented their food," said Mr. Kiberi. When asked how long ago it was, he said it was twelve ancestors ahead.

“My father told me to hold the land firmly and do anything to retain our land.”

He told the elders that he could claim all the land here from all the clans in the community because his father told him that they were the first to arrive here. "My father told me to defend the land in our hands although all the land belongs to us. He told me not to force people into migration, using that as an excuse. He also told me not to take any land from the people using traditional customs. Still, he told me not to let anybody take the land from my hands or any family member because we are the rightful owners of all the land around and beyond," said Mr. Kiberi.

All the elders, who were present, looked at Mr. Kiberi in surprise. Then, one elder was heard whispering to the other, "What Mr. Kiberi is saying is true; all the land belongs to their family because from the ethnic source, they were the first people to settle here. I also heard this from my grandfather, who taught me in his hut when I came from looking after our goats in the field," one of Mr. Kiberi's friends said. "I always joined my grandfather in the evening around his fireplace, where he always told me many things.”

“You are younger in age but older in mind because of what I have taught you. I have seen that you can remember most of the things I tell you and I am happy. However, you will be left to tell your father who knows less than you know because of poor interaction with knowledgeable people and elders," my grandfather used to advise. At this juncture, there was total silence around the Chief's Court. The darkness was almost falling, and the wild animals would be heard from far, testing the time. A little breeze welcoming the evening had started blowing. Mr. Adhamu, Mr. Mindame, and Mr. Kindiana remained silent, watching the ensuing turn of events. Finally, there was enough murmur to show people's dissatisfaction. Even after lighting the fire, nothing was being resolved in the many cases that were taking place.

***

Mr. Matondu and his advocate were afraid when they heard what Mr. Kiberi confessed before the chief's elders. Some of the advocates, who were hired by Mr. Matondu, were afraid to present their views before the chief's court because of what they heard from Mr. Kiberi. But on the other hand, some supported Mr. Matondu. This is because they knew about the land but were 'bought' to present themselves before the court to cover the truth and defeat justice.

When it came to the turn of Nzemba Thirina to tell his story, most of the people were unable to stand and tell this story before him because he narrated how Mr. Kiberi had acquired the land. He said Mr. Kimeri's lineage could possess all the land if they wanted because, according to the tradition, all the land in their community and neighbouring community belonged to their clan. After all, they were the first people to arrive and occupy that land. And when they arrived and occupied that land, they found only wild animals and bushes. Therefore, their land has no boundary from East to West and from North to South. It is only the ocean that can be a boundary to their land! It was known from Mzee Thirina that anyone, who wanted to compete on land ownership with Kiberi's clan, was trying to split a strand of hair with an axe! Therefore, Mzee Thirina advised people to be careful not to lose what they were holding while looking for more.

"It is good that Mr. Kiberi has been advised by his father not to take land from people through cases involving elders. People may take the traditional oath and die because of property. You young people get initiated into the Amakia council of elders. You are like a rat trapped in a gourd when you are not initiated. The rat has nothing to decide on itself. Its entire fate is in the hands of the trapper or the owner of the gourd," said Nzemba Thirina.

"My good children, take my word well and seriously to escape the wrath confronting you and your children. I am the setting sun, and you are the rising sun. Therefore, may I ask you to take my word seriously for your future life and that of your children?" added Nzemba Thirina.

"My days here are almost over, I am enjoying my bonus, and that is why I praise the Omulilo to keep you and your offspring well together with your livestock which is your source of wealth and food," said Mzee Thirina.

Most of the advocates and elders, who were present, and had come to say what they knew of the land and Mr. Matondu, were so afraid to speak as if Nzemba Thirina was a god in that case. "I am ready to take the traditional oath to support what I have said about that land. I am not in favour of anybody before this court. Instead, I am standing for the truth from my grandfather Mnande," said Nzemba Thirina. He then sat onto the circle facing the elders and the parties in dispute.

Some spokesmen talked in favour of Mr. Matondu. However, people started guessing the truth when Mr. Kiberi and his advocate, Nzemba Thirina, spoke about what they knew about the land from their grandfathers and ancestors. Everybody was again in fear when they heard that all the land belonged to the clan of Mr. Kiberi. His father advised against asking for it unless he was defending his land against others, like in the present case.

Most of the advocates and spokesmen were afraid that Mr. Kiberi might forget or ignore his father's advice and ask for their portion of the land. So, many elders and witnesses were forced to keep quiet against contribution in that case in favour of Mr. Matondu.

Some of the chief's elders knew the truth. However, they could not stop the case from proceeding because that would also stop the payment of the fees which catered for their labour in the court. Again, it could mean denying justice to the other party, who were ready to continue their case to fruition before the chief's court where elders were practicing traditional law.

The two parties addressed the chief's court until they were exhausted. Unlike before, when people, especially the advocates and spokespersons, asked questions, there were no questions this time. There was just a single question that was asked by Mr. Minata from the Randu clan. He asked Mr. Kiberi whether he knew the boundary of their clan land. All the people inside the chief's court looked at one another inquisitively. Mr. Kiberi looked at the chief's appointee, who was also the chairman of the court.

"Mr. Kiberi, answer the question," the chairman implored.

"Mr. Chairman, the boundary of that land he is asking about is all the land in the seven communities or clans: the land in the clan of Karima, Randu, Sekali, Tabu, Urange, Bembu, and Malange. All this land is supposed to be mine, but my father refused me to say so. I am not supposed to say so. That is why you have forced and prompted me to say that publicly. And the chief's appointee has also asked me to answer you," answered Mr. Kiberi.

Everybody in the court wondered whether all that land belonged to Mr. Kiberi's clan. It meant that the six clans had occupied their land without rightful ownership. This land could be claimed using the traditional law and constitution.

People in the court started murmuring when they realised that their houses, the land which was their food source, belonged to Kiberi and his clan. They feared that the Kiberis might claim the land one day in their lifetime or after their lifetime, leaving them impoverished because without the land, which many refer to as 'their mother,' they would all perish.

Many people started wondering whether an individual or a clan could hold other people at ransom. Others were afraid and conceived that the whole community consisted of seven clans living at the mercy of one clan or a person. This was worrisome since one person could stand up and proclaim the land, take it and own it solely. This person was Mr. Kiberi, son of Mbilongo. After this revelation, all the people in the court fell silent. Everybody, including the chairman, was amazed by the claim that one clan owned the whole land occupied by six clans by invoking the traditional law, historical knowledge, and other cultural forces.

The court chairman was at crossroads as to whether to call other spokesmen to contribute or either side of the case or call for a private session of the conversant elders. However, the answer to the dispute was almost obvious. The court elders asked whether there was anyone else who would like to testify on either side of the case before they concluded and not the major parties in dispute.

All the people murmured without saying a word to either support or dispute. The court chairman called Mr. Matondu to conclude his case and explain why he believed the land belonged to him, especially since their relatives were working on that land. He was asked by one of the court elders whether he would face traditional cultural law to justify his statement. When this question of oath or the cultural law arose, he developed cold feet. He did not oblige to take since he knew the consequences of the oath. Instead, he insisted that he had been working on that plot long enough. Finally, Mr. Kiberi was asked to conclude his statement before the court. After a few minutes of silence, he said he was ready to face any traditional customary and cultural oath or law. He was ready to face any punishment to take back the land. He asked the chief's elders to administer the 'he-goat' oath to Mr. Matondu to justify the ownership of the plot.

When Mr. Matondu was asked whether he was ready to have the 'he-goat' oath to possess his alleged land, he said he had one more advocate, Mr. Mulama, who had to come and testify before the case was concluded. The chief's elders were requested to bring him so that he could take the oath. The chief requested the elders to look for him and bring him before the court.

The cases went in circles on this day, and nothing much was achieved. Finally, the sun had gone down, and the elders had become exhausted. The chief stood up, looked in the sun's direction, and said, "The sun has gone to sleep."

"We cannot proceed with cases tonight. No case can be heard or determined in the darkness. Therefore, the Chief's Court is adjourned." He concluded and stamped his staff on the ground. The Chief had spoken. Nothing else could be said unless one wanted to be slapped with a rebuke and fine. When the Chief spoke, it was final. The people and their spokespersons dispersed in different directions heading to their homes. The case was postponed to another day to wait for Mr. Matondu's witness, who would give testimony as the last one. Before the elders left, the witness of Mr. Matondu's case had to meet and discuss issues of importance and what they would do to win the case. Five of them, including Mr. Matondu himself, had promised to meet outside the Chief's court compound to chat the way forward. The others suggested that they should meet at home to discuss what they should do. Mr. Matondu was asked to suggest the day his supporters or witnesses would meet and finalise their defence from home. Other elders suggested that they should be allowed time to mobilise more elders who were experienced in the law of the land. Mr. Matondu committed with his close family members and agreed that they should meet on the following Thursday at Matondu's home at around 10.00 o'clock in the morning to plan what to do, and all the elders, who were in court, should be present on that day.

Chapter Four

The next day cases were opened early enough. Many other cases were to be listened to and determined on the same day as Matondu's. The other few cases that were to be listened to by the chief's elders included: the destruction of food crops, livestock, child ownership between two men who both had an affair with the child's mother, the debt of a bull, payment of dowry and inheritance of a cow between two brothers whose father had passed away.

On that day, only three cases were listened to and concluded. The other three were postponed to the following day for the time factor. The Chief explained to the parties that they would listen early the following day. He, therefore, requested the elders to show up before the sun stood on their faces. This could be after the birds had woken up and settled from their first feeding from the trees.

He also explained that the cases would be listened to in order of priority, and if the parties were not ready, the next party would be listened to. The chairman told them that he would start with the case of Mr. Aboru, whose cows were alleged to have destroyed the food crops of Mr. Abweri at Murakima in the Walange clan.

The next case involved Mr. Adima and Ngemwe over the ownership of a child born outside marriage.

The Chief requested the parties to be strictly present early enough because the elders would be ready. He advised them to make thorough and proper preparation for that day, and if possible, they should spend the night together before the day of the case. All the parties in those cases had to make a consultation to gather points for their defence and arguments. Others consulted because they wanted to organise themselves for a late lunch. Some elders had promised something to take home to the family at the end of the cases. Maybe, they knew they would have something from those whose cases were being heard. Others wanted to go and discuss the cases in public gatherings such as bars or *ajua* playing places. One old man, called Mr. Ngemwe, had talked to his elders before they broke away and arranged to meet them at home for further discussion. One of the elders advised others to look for an elder who conversed with traditional and cultural matters to tackle the cases correctly. "Let us look for other two or three elders to be able to discuss the issue exhaustively and know the direction we are taking before the day of the case," advised Mr. Ngemwe.

The elders agreed that they must meet at around noon at Ngemwe's home for more consultation and discussion. Mr. Ngemwe's brother, Mr. Murema, advised the elders to research the cases facing them from other experienced persons or elders before that day. "Experience and knowledge are very good tools for solving problems, especially cases of this nature," he advised. Mr. Murema consulted with his brother to see what would happen that day. "We must be prepared at home before we go to the Chief's court for the case. We should be able to know how many people we expect at your home and what they will eat and drink. We need to know who they are so that we can inform our close relatives. This looks more or less a family matter," he said again.

They agreed that the preparation should be there to chart the way forward. They also should list down who should be invited to the discussion. Mr. Murema called his brother aside, and they agreed on what should be done that day. Mr. Ngemwe and his brother Murema went home and started preparations for the following Monday. They prepared all that was needed for that Monday. When Ngemwe reached his home, he summoned his wife and explained to her what he wanted to be prepared for the following Monday. "We have elders coming here on Monday, and I have already sent for them, and I'm sending for others. That case is not as simple as some of us may think. Elders, who are well-versed with the traditional laws and are members of Amakia, will discuss it. I have also invited them on that day here, and we shall be able to know how to approach the issue. I have sent for members of the Amakia council of elders from different clans. I have one from Wame, Mr. Mberi, Mr. Meti from Shalu, Mr. Neka from Yawelo and Mr. Thiamu from Zambila among others. Apart from these elders, I have invited others who are well-experienced with this community's traditional laws and culture," said Mr. Ngemwe.

Within a short while, his brother Murema arrived at Mr. Ngemwe's compound and met him, discussed the occasion with his wife, and greeted them. Naturally, they responded to the greetings. "We are arranging and discussing those occasions with Mumika, and I have explained to her what is expected on Monday," said Mr. Ngemwe.

They sat with his brother and made arrangements about the said Monday before approaching Wednesday, the day of the case. Then, Mr. Ngemwe opened the house, where he invited his brother for further discussion about the occasion. After that, they sat inside the house and spent some time discussing the occasion's program. Murema's wife also arrived and joined the other woman in preparing and drawing the programme. They also sat down and discussed many areas that needed to be addressed to make the occasion a success.

They had to plan for about ten people, the food needed on that day, and as Amwaria, they would have drinks because in Amwaria tradition, elders take drinks in discussions of that nature, and that is what pleases them. Therefore, there was a need to prepare drinks. Ngemwe's wife went where. The two brothers were seated and asked about the kind of drinks to take that day. He consulted his brother, and they agreed the drink would be honey and some tea, which would be taken by two or three people.

Mr. Ngemwe told the wife to plan for food because he would know how the honey would be prepared. "What of tea?" asked the wife. "This is like normal tea we take here in the morning; three people wouldn't take much; tea is cheap to prepare," responded Mr. Ngemwe. The two brothers discussed how the honey was to be prepared. Mr. Murema promised to donate six kilograms of honey for that day. He had harvested the honey from his beehive the previous week and had two full drums. He also offered dried Mulombe fruits to act as catalysts when the honey beer was prepared. They agreed that the honey beer should mature for two to three days. "Three days' honey beer is strong; some elders may not be able to get to their homes after taking it,' said Mr. Murema. "We can prepare another honey to adulterate the former one in case it is stronger than we expect," said his brother Mr. Ngemwe. His brother nodded in agreement. Mr. Murema summoned his wife where they were seated and asked her whether the honey he had harvested could reach there the same day or the following day in the morning. "May I try and see whether it can be brought here today and at latest tomorrow at 8.00 a.m.?" she responded.

They both agreed that the honey beer should be prepared on Saturday morning by an experienced person in a pot of about forty litres, and by Monday morning, that brew should be mature enough to be taken by elders.

"Do you have enough dry Mulombe fruits which will facilitate the beer to be mature in two days, Mr. Murema?" asked Ngemwe. "I have enough Mulombe fruit catalyst for even six big pots in my house. Others are borrowed by people to prepare their beer for occasions and personal use," responded Murema.

Ngemwe's wife had already programmed the food that would be eaten on that day. Black beans, green vegetables, sweet potatoes, and bananas would serve as lunch. There were six cocks and several hens in her house. They could be used to serve as meat. Two cocks were enough because the cocks were at least two and a half kilogrammes each.

If the husband insisted that he wanted cow's or goat's meat, this could be provided from the market on Saturday and could be preserved with salt to wait for Monday's occasion. There were enough utensils, plates, spoons, sufurias, kettles, and other household goods to serve the visitors. There was firewood in the compound for that purpose. This means all the major areas of the occasion were catered for. The only areas they had not prepared for were the men's drink which fell under the catering of the men's department according to the arrangement.

When they were discussing the issue, the arrangement for men's drink was arranged from the men's side, and all was completed. Very early the following morning, Mrs. Murema sent her son to Ngemwe with six kilogrammes of honey in a closed can. This was even before Mrs. Ngwemwe had prepared morning tea.

Mrs. Ngemwe saw the boy holding a can in his hand. He greeted Mrs. Ngemwe in the traditional language. “Good morning, aunt,” greeted master Alemi. “Good morning, master Alemi," responded Mrs. Ngemwe. "I have been sent to you with this tin. I was given it last night by my mother. She packed it at around 8.30 p.m., asked me to deliver it very early in the morning, and directed me not to wait for tea at home. She told me to disappear from the compound when the morning was clear, and I took it seriously. My father told my mother to bring it before 8:00 a.m., which is why I am here,” said Alemi.

Mrs. Ngemwe took the small container and opened it. She dipped her right finger into the can and licked. "This is pure honey from the beehive, and it has not stayed for long since it was harvested," said Mrs. Mwema. "My father and another old man Mr. Gigali, who accompanies my father while going to harvest, brought it from harvesting on Thursday at around 9.30 p.m. as we were preparing to go and sleep," said Alemi. Mrs. Ngemwe took the can and kept it inside her house, where other foodstuffs were usually kept. She asked Alemi to sit down and wait for the tea to be ready. Alemi was interested to see the pigs which were enclosed in their pigsty in the compound and always wanted to hear the noises they made. So he went next to the enclosure. "Don't stay there for long because they are expecting their breakfast when they see you near their house because I feed them around this time," said Mrs. Ngemwe. "They think you have something for their belly," added Mrs. Ngemwe as she prepared tea. Alemi moved from the pigsty to the cows' shed.

His uncle Mr. Ngemwe had kept all kinds of livestock in his home. There were goats, cows, pigs, rabbits, and chickens. Some cows grazed out in the field, and some were under zero grazing. They did not dwell in the same area. Those, which grazed out in the fields, were next to the pigsty and those, which were under zero grazing, were around the chicken compound. There was a store next to each livestock house with food for that kind of livestock, drugs, and chemicals. But chemicals were kept in a wooden box which was tightly closed and kept in a separate corner.

Eight cows grazed in the field, and three zero-grazing cows were in the cows' shed. Two zero-grazing cows were milking, and there was a bull that was almost the size of a buffalo. There were one hundred and twenty chickens in three different places. There were exotic and local chickens. There was a store with several logs of wood and a water tank next to the store. The store was tightly locked with a padlock to prevent anybody without authority from getting access.

In the goats' shed, there were ten goats, three he-goats, and seven she-goats. Among them, three young ones sucked their mother. The three he-goats were kept in two different feeding places. The exotic one was kept among the exotic breeds, and the two local breeds were kept among their breed. One big he-goat was making mating noise. The noise was so loud that even the owner said they could not sleep well the previous nights since it started mating some three days ago.

Mr. Ngemwe had castrated the other one when it disturbed the whole compound while mating. The owner also said it was always fighting the others while in a mating state.

In the chickens' coop, there were chickens with chicks. There were as many as sixty of them. The rabbits were secluded next to the chickens, and there were as many as ten of them in their pen. There was also a store next to their pen. The store was loaded with their food, and mindreine was applied to them at different times of the year. Alemi had gone round all the areas where the livestock was kept. He also went around the chicken area and visited all the animals' buildings. His uncle had woken up after his name-sake Alemi had brought a can of honey. He called him when he asked his wife who had brought the honey. "Alemi," his uncle called him. "I am visiting the livestock area," responded Alemi.

"Come and take tea, and then you will come to visit what you want to see at the animals' place," said his uncle, Ngemwe. Alemi came to the place where his name-sake was standing next to the kitchen looking in the direction of the kitchen. "When did you arrive, Alemi?" his uncle asked. "My mother packed the honey for me at around 9.30 p.m. last night and asked me to bring it as early as possible, even before taking morning tea. She told me to make sure I bring it here and deliver it to my aunt," he responded.

Alemi followed his uncle into the house where his cousins were waiting for breakfast. They all greeted Alemi happily, and he sat next to his cousins at the table. Within a short time, Mrs. Ngemwe came in with tea in one hand and ripe roasted bananas in the other on a serving plate. She asked her son whether he had greeted his cousins, and he responded in the affirmative. "This is Alemi, my brother's son and my name-sake," said Mr. Ngemwe to his children. "This is the second time he's coming here," said Mrs. Ngemwe to her husband. Mrs. Ngemwe went to the next house and brought drinking glasses and cups. She also brought bread smeared with honey.

They all sat at the table and took tea together. Mr. Ngemwe took tea with roasted bananas from exotic banana breeds. She asked her children to eat roasted bananas, but they chose to take tea and honey-smeared bread and bananas. Mrs. Ngemwe also took bread and ripe bananas. There was Pin drop silence. When they were having breakfast, the cousins fixed their eyes on Alemi. Mr. Ngemwe asked Alemi to take tea well and not as slowly as he was doing. His uncle took the kettle with tea and added some tea to Alemi's glass.

Mr. Ngemwe added tea to those who had almost finished and those who had finished. He did not add to his wife's glass. She came to add to her own glass after a few minutes. "Take tea well so I can bring more in the sufuria."

"Can you be added some milk, or do you take milk alone?" Ngemwe asked Alemi. Alemi kept quiet and did not answer. He felt shy about what his uncle asked him. He did not want to answer the question. He covered his mouth with his right hand shyly. His uncle asked his wife to serve him with a glass of milk. He was given milk and kept next to his glass of tea. His aunt asked him to take the milk or mix it with tea in front of him.

They cleared from the table when they were done with taking tea. His uncle asked his wife to get a cock and give it to Alemi as a gift. So Mrs. Ngemwe went to the chicken's house, got hold of the medium cock of local breed, and tied its legs with a sisal rope. She brought it to her husband to present to his name-sake. Mr. Ngemwe took the cock and proclaimed it fit.

He called his nephew and name-sake to where he was seated and gave him the cock. "Take this cock as a gift from me. This is now yours," said Mr. Ngemwe to Alemi. So the boy took the cock and left for home.

Chapter Five

The people invited started trickling in slowly. The head of the family, where the meeting was due to take place, was in the compound. He was headed to the main house. But, before he could enter the main house, Mr. Ndime entered his compound accompanied by another old man.

They shouted greetings at him. "Good morning, Nzemba Ndime," they greeted. "Good morning to you elders, welcome," Nzemba Ngali answered, turning back to see who was greeting him. They approached him and shook hands. The old man was carrying something tied in a bundle with a green plastic bag. Mr. Murema, who had accompanied Mr. Ndimwe, took the bundle to the old man, who opened it a little. "This honey is enough for my pot," the family owner said excitedly.

"Yes, I got the best for you. This honey is ripe. It will make people drunk very fast," Mr. Murema said. "If you start the brew now, it will be ready in twenty hours," Mr. Ndimwe bragged. "You have to check the brew in twenty hours, or else it will be over-ripe," Mr. Murema added. The old man, Mr. Gigali, nodded in appreciation.

Mr. Gigali was also a specialist in preparing *oli* drinks.

Mr. Murema went to the house where the honey was to be prepared with the two colleagues, Mr. Ndime and Mr. Gigali. Mr. Murema called his wife to prepare the pot for brewing the honey. His wife came fast and entered the house. She brought a pot ready to be used to prepare the *oliro* brew. Her husband showed her where to place it in the main house. Then, she was asked to prepare water for the elders. She was advised to fill in about sixty-five litres of water in the pot.

When water was ready, she called her husband, and the husband alerted Mr. Gigali and Mr. Ndime. The water was put in the pot, and Mr. Ndime got some honey, mixed it with hot water, and stirred a bit. The mixture of the two was then poured into the pot with the water. Mr. Gigali tasted the concentration of the drink from the pot and said that more honey should be added to concentrate it. He took a cup, got some honey, added some water, and stirred. He then poured it into the beer pot. He tasted again and confirmed that the honey beer was concentrated. The pot was properly fixed with three stones which supported the pot to stand more firmly. Muratĩna catalysts were tied together in a bundle and were eight in number. The pot was covered with green banana leaves to prevent anything from entering the pot.

Mr. Gigali rubbed his hands together and commented, "This beer should be ready by tomorrow afternoon. It should be checked before that time, and if it is ready, more honey should be stirred and added to the beer pot to enable it to be taken early on Monday." "That is okay," added Ndime. "When it is ready, half a litre will be enough for a person, and more than that would be disastrous to the takers of that beer," added Mr. Ndime.

Mr. Ngemwe appeared as the three wanted to leave the house. “Are you through?" asked Mr. Ngemwe. "Yes, about ten hours, and the beer would be a very strong drink. Make sure the children do not tamper with this pot," directed Mr. Ngemwe to his wife. They left the house for the gate, and before they reached it, they stopped near the cattle shed to discuss an issue as the day was getting near. Mr. Ngemwe asked Mr. Ndime to come and check whether the beer would be ready by the next day and what would happen to those who were waiting. He even asked both of them to come for that day. He told them to ask his wife for the fresh honey in case they wanted to concentrate or de-concentrate the drink.

They all agreed to meet the following day to know the state of the beer. Mr. Ngemwe had organised the old men who were ready for the case and who would meet on Monday to prepare the case, which would be heard on Wednesday between Mr. Ngemwe and Mr. Adima before the chief's elders at the chief's office ground. The old man and Ngemwe’s advocates were to meet at his home to prepare for the case.

On Monday morning, many people had come to Mr. Ngemwe's home; some had come to prepare the food and drinks for the visitors. Other members, who had come to welcome the visitors, were family friends. Some relatives had come to accompany the visitors. On Sunday afternoon, Mr. Gigali came to Ngemwe's home at around 5.00 p.m. and knocked at the gate. The child told her mother that somebody was knocking at the gate, and the mother walked towards the gate. Mrs. Ngemwe opened the gate and saw Mr. Gigali standing at the gate. After exchanging greetings, Gigali took some steps into the compound, sauntering to allow Mrs. Ngemwe, who had been left behind minding the gate, to catch up with him.

"Mrs. Ngemwe, where is your husband?" asked Gigali.

"He left after lunch and told me to wait for you to check on the drink for tomorrow's occasion," responded Mrs. Ngemwe. She led Mr. Gigali to the room where the honey beer was, and bubbling sounds could be heard from the pot that contained the brew.

Mr. Gigali took off the pot's lid. He asked for a metallic cup and tasted the honey beer. "This is a strong beer and good. But, for now, it must be adulterated for readiness for the next seventeen hours," said Gigali.

“Hand me honey and hot water to de-concentrate the honey beer for tomorrow’s occasion,” he added.

“What amount of hot water?” asked Mrs. Ngemwe.

“Bring the quantity of a quarter of a calabash we used when I was preparing yesterday,” answered Gigali.

Mrs. Ngemwe went outside to prepare the hot water she was asked to bring, and within twenty minutes, she returned with a calabash of hot water. Mr. Gigali asked her for a wooden jug. She brought the wooden jug with a lid. He removed the lid, poured some honey beer into the wooden jug, and then replaced the lid. He asked Mr. Ngemwe to bring the calabash for her drink share, and Mr. Ngemwe said women were not supposed to take beer prepared for old men's occasions, especially when discussing an important issue. That taboo was right and well-informed in the traditional custom of the Amunge society.

"Take this jug and give it to your husband when he returns," said Gigali.

He took honey, stirred it with a wooden spoon, and then poured it into the pot which had prepared the beer. Next, he reduced the mulombe catalyst, put them in the sufuria, and left others in the beer pot. Finally, he took another cup and covered the pot.

"I will come in the morning to check it the last time before the beer is presented to the elders to drink."

He went outside the house and was escorted by Mr. Ngemwe to the gate. Before they reached the gate, they heard another knock on the gate. They proceeded to the gate, where they met Mr. Ngemwe. Mrs. Ngemwe opened the gate.

"Oh, Mr. Gigali, you came," said Mr. Ngemwe.

"Yes, I did, just as we had agreed yesterday," responded Gigali.

"Let us go back and say more for tomorrow," Ngemwe said to Gigali.

Mrs. Ngemwe closed the gate and followed them behind. She opened the house where the honey beer was prepared, and they all entered. Mr. Gigali explained what he had done to the honey beer. He opened the pot for Ngemwe to see the quantity of beer and what he had done.

They left for Ngemwe's living house, and after they had taken their seats, Murema brought the honey beer Gigali had spared for Ngemwe to sample. She also brought two wooden cups. Ngemwe filled the two cups with honey beer and took his cup to taste. He took another sip, and he was not speaking to Gigali.

"How is it?" asked Gigali.

"This is a strong beer, and the old men and the advocates may drink and forget the purpose of coming because of its alcoholic content," responded Ngemwe. Mr. Gigali told Mr. Ngemwe that they knew why they were coming and how they would conduct themselves, and they also expected there were drink and the effect of the drink.

"They should start with discussion as the food is prepared and served, with a little honey beer as they talk. They know themselves and the beer when discussing an important issue like this one," explained Mr. Gigali. They took the honey beer brought by the wife, and Mr. Gigali turned down a second cup since he had tasted the beer earlier. He told Mr. Ngemwe that he could not take more honey beer because he might be unable to carry himself to his compound for the night. Mr. Ngemwe took another two wooden cups and confessed that the honey beer was strong.

“Honey beer is not like the ordinary gruel prepared by our wives,” said Ngemwe to Mr. Gigali.

"It has a strong alcoholic effect after drinking and entering into the blood system," added Ngemwe.

“I totally agree with you,” said Mr. Gigali.

Mr. Gigali told Ngemwe how he had taken honey beer some three years back from his friend's house, Mr. Dakala from Urange, and he was about to be washed away by floods on his way home. "I was helped by a woman who shouted for help, and young people came and saved me and took me to their home where I spent the night. I did not realise where I was until the next morning at 5.00 a.m. When my ordeal was explained to me, I could hardly believe it. So, honey beer should not be taken lightly. You take it, and not only do you forget what you are likely to contribute, but you forget yourself and those around you," said Mr. Gigali.

Mr. Ngemwe said there should be an order of taking and talking, and they were aware of this because that was not the first day to take honey beer while discussing issues of that nature. They all agreed that the elders and advocates are grown-ups and mature people. Mr. Gigali said he would come the next day very early to see the state of the beer and other ground preparation before the meeting took off. Since it was getting late at night, Mr. Gigali asked Mr. Ngemwe to allow him to head home.

"The two cups of this beer I have taken are working against my sobriety. I can feel the effect only after the few minutes I have taken. I need to rush home and make sure I am near my bed. Let us not extend the discussions, Mr. Ngemwe. Please rush me to your gate and bid me goodbye,” said Mr. Gigali.

"I agree with you, Gigali; alcohol is not milk," added Ngemwe as he prepared to escort him to the gate. He then walked him to the gate and wished him goodbye.

“See you tomorrow, Mr. Gigali,” said Ngemwe.

“And you too,” said Mr. Gigali.

***

Before he left for his home, Mr. Ngemwe had asked him not to stop anywhere on the way before he reached home. He had told him to go home straight and not to stop on the way talking to anybody because he needed to sleep early to be able to report to his house the following day. Mr. Gigali knew the effect of honey beer and took Ngemwe's instructions seriously. He kept walking until he reached his compound, and after getting there, he asked his wife Ngila to open the gate for him. Ngila sent one of her sons, Kalu, to go and open the gate for his father. Kalu ran up to the gate quickly and opened the gate for his father. The time was about 8.30 p.m.

Master Kalu told his father they were asking where he was because it was becoming dark, and they were worried when they heard screaming in the neighbouring village. He told the father that his mother was asking about his whereabouts. Mr. Gigali told his son that he was held up at Ngemwe's home preparing for an occasion to take place the following Monday, and they had sat to discuss and prepare issues and programme, respectively.

He went to his house and sat next to his young son as his wife was preparing dinner. "We were worried when we heard screams from the neighbouring village, and I was worried because you were not anywhere to be seen. The social surroundings and environment are changing, not necessarily for the better; it may even change for the worse. My grandmother Chilumi used to call darkness a blanket for the thieves. When we were seated in her house, she used to tell us stories and concluded by telling us to avoid the thieves' blanket. You should also try to avoid the thief's blanket for your good," concluded Ngila.

Mr. Gigali told his wife why he was late. He told her that men could be late for many things, not necessarily for their own benefits but for other people's social and material benefits. "My friend, Mr. Ngemwe, has invited his advocates tomorrow at his home, and I was preparing the honey beer for them and other programmes. So I am arranging all these, especially the honey beer, to be taken that day. And therefore, I have been forced to be late to overcome the failure of the occasion," added Mr. Gigali.

The wife complained about his social state before even the children. "Everybody in this house can see that your social state has changed, which is why the children are quiet and just listening to what you are saying. They can see that your behaviour has completely changed. You entered the house staggering, holding onto the door for support and staggering when sitting. That has surprised the children for the first time," complained Ngila.

She took the wooden spoon and lit the fire to prepare food for the family, which was ready. But, before Ngila prepared and shared the food, her husband was preparing to go to bed. "Eat first and then go to bed," she told him.

He struggled and left for his bed in his house. She followed him and made sure he had traced the bed and slept. Then, she left for her house to prepare the food and serve her children. She complained about the attitude and behaviour of her husband but was not sharing with the children what she said. Instead, she kept it to herself.

She shared the food with the children. She then prepared the fire for her husband, put the food on the wooden plate, and took it to him. She woke him, but he could not wake up and take food. She took the food back and took her share. She went and closed the door for him from outside. She was very angry with her husband's behaviour and drunkenness.

She prepared the beds for her children because it was getting late and the young children were dozing. She took the young children to their respective beds and made sure she covered them with blankets in their separate beds. Then, she went out with a wooden flame torch and checked whether all the cows were present and secure in their enclosures. Ngila went to her house, closed the door, and slept for the night. The main gate was locked safely, the doors to the houses were closed, and the home rested for the night to await the break of the day.

Chapter Six

At 4.30 a.m., Mr. Gigali woke up and discovered that the door to his house was locked from the outside and not the usual inside. He wondered what had happened as that was unusual in his home. He tried to reason how it had occurred that the door was locked from outside but could not get an answer to the question. He tried to recall how he came to his home and got into his bed but was still in the darkness. He had no fire to light. He was alone in the house. He reasoned that it would be shameful to call his wife loudly and to make matters worse, it was dead in the night when everybody was asleep. He shook the wooden door and discovered that it was tightly locked.

He blindly staggered from his bed and, at times, stepped on the sleeping goats and their young ones. He cared not to step on the young kids and kill or injure them. He bent down and crept to avoid stepping on the young kids and finally traced the support of his wooden bed. He stood up, sat back on his bed, and finally slept again. He could no longer sleep and remained awake for the remainder of the night. As he was on the bed, eyes open, he heard the cock crow and guessed the time of the night. He heard another cock crow in the upper direction. He silently said, "That is Mr. Rabiana's cock." He knew that the day was almost opening, and his sleepless state would be a thing of the past. He heard the other two cocks crow in different directions and almost simultaneously. He also heard birds chirping in the nearby bush and trees making noise. He was sure the day was almost breaking.

After the birds chirping, he heard people talking in the distance and knew it was already morning hours. When he peeped through a small hole in the wall of his house, he could see the light outside, but he was not free to awake his wife because he knew all was not well with her. He knew his wife did not like a person who forgets himself under the influence of alcohol. He knew that she had noticed, and she was most likely the one who locked the house from outside or instructed another person to do so.

Mr. Gigali wanted to call his wife to come and open for him, but he was weighed down by guilt. As the birds sang, the light increased, giving birth to a new day. Mr. Gigali had not shut his eyes since he awoke at around four. He felt like going for a short call, but this too was not possible, and again he could not have done so inside the house because taboo restricted him. When the time came for Ngila to milk the cows, she opened the door of her house, went towards the house where the husband slept, and started opening it from outside. Gigali was awake and waiting for her to open, and then he could take a short call outside. When she opened, she called, "Gigali, Gigali, where are you?" Gigali was filled with guilt conscious and could not respond immediately though he was awake and wanted to go outside to take a short call. He had not covered himself with a blanket but had merely stretched himself on the bed.

Ngila entered the house to check why Gigali was not responding and whether he was still asleep because of his not responding to the several calls she made. When Gigali heard his wife's footsteps, the bed made creaking noises as Gigali was trying to rise up. "Did you sleep uncovered for the whole night?" she asked. Gigali did not give an immediate answer because he was not prepared for that kind of question. "No, I had covered myself, but I slept when I was tired from yesterday's walk and other exercises during the day," said Gigali as he was trying to awake from the bed. "Were you tired from the exercise you did, or were you drunk?" asked Ngila angrily.

"Are you drunk when tired, or are you tired when you are drunk?" asked Gigali to minimise questions from his wife, who was not happy with his social behaviour the previous night. She hesitated to answer the question, noting that the question was not a friendly and co-operative one. She knew when the husband was hungry, he spoke rudely and uncooperatively. "And where did you eat last night because you refused our food and slept without taking dinner?" asked Ngila. "Is that why you locked me from outside? What if the house caught fire? What could have happened? Is that what you were educated by your people before I married you and especially your grandmother and your mother? That is unheard of!" lamented Gigali.

Ngila did not say a word. She disappeared to her house, and Gigali went outside behind his house for a short call. Ngila tried to fix the cow to its place and started milking. Gigali could hear the sound of milking from where he stood outside the house after attending to a short call. To surprise Ngila and suppress her feelings, Gigali said, "This is unheard in the world of men. Women can create your hell; I spent the night as if I was in a white man's prison; if a fire broke out, I would burn to ashes because my father Daru and my mother Enoki were not there to open for me!" He was saying that within hearing distance from his wife, whom he was educating with such statements to comfort himself. Ngila milked all the cows and started preparing morning tea.

Mr. Gigali went near the main house where Ngila was preparing tea and asked for his panga. "Who took the panga from my house yesterday because I left it there at noon? It was kept next to my bed," commented Gigali. Ngila briefly abandoned preparing tea and took the panga, which was taken to cut firewood by the children. She handed it over to him. Mr. Gigali went towards the direction of the gate, opened it, walked out, then closed it behind him. He went to his banana plantation to cut fodder for his goats. He also took banana leaves for the young calves. He dropped them in the compound.

He went the second time and cut the banana trunks for the mother cows and other adults. Then, he went and opened the enclosures where the cows were enclosed. They rushed to take the breakfast Mr. Gigali had prepared for them. Mr. Gigali also prepared the places for goats where he had placed their feed, took them from his house where they slept, and enclosed them in their day feeding pens.

Mr. Gigali started preparing the fence from the gate. He was almost wet on his feet and his trouser because there were dews on the plants he was cutting to feed his animals. His wife could see but could not comment because she understood his comment that morning. Ngila took that comment seriously and questioned herself, especially about locking the house from the outside and the emergency of fire. She was also afraid to be taken before her relatives to answer the issues.

"Gigali is right; my mother can put me into trouble if I'm accused before my father of what I did last night. But I was doing it in a clean heart to safeguard the goats, and he was drunk," Ngila said silently in her heart. That was her defence if Gigali accused her before her parents. Ngila was happy with her husband that morning. "Come for tea," said Ngila to Gigali. She took tea to his house with a jug, warmed the food he had not taken the previous night, and kept it in a place that goats could not reach. She went outside. Gigali came to the house and started taking his meal.

He remembered the night and vowed not to repeat the thing again. He even felt bad because his wife was not happy with the behaviour. The wife was also not satisfied because she did not like the children to see what the father was doing under the effect of alcohol. The children had not experienced such a state of their father, and the mother did not like to disclose it to them. Mr. Gigali knew his wife as a good wife who corrected bad things to educate the children and bring them up as useful and good-mannered people before her community and the clan. However, he knew his wife disapproved of the state he was in the previous night.

"The black cow is sick or has eaten something which is affecting its health; it has been quiet and has been sleeping since it came, and it was not moving after its young one when it came from the fields for grazing. The milk I have managed from it today is half of what I usually get. She is not even feeding from the food you have brought now," said Ngila to her husband.

Mr. Gigali looked in the cows' direction. He could not see it, so he went near the feeding place and found it resting and panting. "This is a serious matter; this cow carries the whole family on its shoulders. She is the great grandmother of all these other cows here except one, which was paid as dowry for my sister. All others have descended from her," said Mr. Gigali. He rushed to the neighbour who grazed with him alternatively, Mr. Kemalo. The two families were grazing every three days, and Kemalo's son Mundeti was the one grazing the cows the previous day.

Mr. Gigali entered Kemalo's compound in a breeze and met Mr. Kemalo taking breakfast near the cows' enclosure. He was talking to his son, Naalo, who was going to graze that day. He greeted Mr. Kemalo using the Amakia council of elders' language because they were both members and greeted his son in the ordinary language. "Bereha haba, Mr. Kemalo," Mr. Gigali greeted Mr. Kemalo. "Bereha haba, Gigali," Mr. Kemalo responded.

"Who was grazing the cows yesterday, and where was he grazing them?" inquired Mr. Gigali. "My son Adiba went with them to Amwende swamp, but let us know where he passed with them on his way to the swamp or from the swamp," responded Mr. Kemalo. He sent for his son, and the mother said he was taking breakfast but was soon coming. He momentarily appeared to be running, pushing a circular ring with his hand. 'I have come, father," he said. "How did you move with animals yesterday from here, and how did you bring them back from the grazing field?" asked the father.

Adiba was surprised by the question and did not immediately know how to answer it. First, he looked at his father. Next, he looked at Mr. Gigali, and finally, he looked at his brother, who was eating a roasted banana. Master Adiba explained how he moved with the animals from home to Mumeko ground. "I stayed with them for about thirty minutes before proceeding to Alembo secondary school, where the school field was opened for people to graze to reduce the size of grass, which had become a bush of its own. There were many cows, but our cows did not mix with other cows grazing there. I then drove them to Amwembe swamp at around 1.00 p.m., and they drank water at the same place. I grazed them there for the rest of the day and drove them home," said master Adiba. "And before I forget, I had a problem with a black cow belonging to Mr. Gigali because it was not feeding almost throughout the day. It even had difficulties walking to and from the field. So I was forced to drive them slowly to reach home safely. There must be something seriously wrong with it. It always leads other cows, but yesterday it was trailing. I was very much doubtful whether it would get here," Adiba told them.

Mr. Gigali had agreed with Adiba about the state of his black cow. "Let us go and see the cow," said Mr. Kemalo. They started leaving, and Adiba asked his father to wait for him to hide the ring on his bed in his mother's house. "Don't delay; I don't want to keep Gigali here." He came running and followed his father until they got to Mr. Gigali's compound. They met Gigali waking it up. When Adiba saw the black cow, he told his father, "That is the cow I told you about; it could not feed well or walk. I had to push it carefully."

"Adiba is a careful young boy while handling and taking care of our livestock. He can very quickly understand their problem and give them an immediate response," said the father to Mr. Gigali. Gigali's children and his wife Ngila came to see why neighbours had come to surround their black cow. "Is the condition worsening?" asked Ngila. "No," responded the husband, "I had gone to Mr. Kemalo's home to know where they were grazing and how they came home to assist me in understanding the real problem," said Mr. Gigali. The family of Mr. Gigali was surprised to learn that the family expectations were dwindling. Even Mr. Gigali had changed his voice and face when he understood the state of their black cow. "Look for managu leaves; make it drink the contents when it is boiled," said Mr. Kemalo. "They are plenty in the surrounding area," added Mr. Kemalo.

Mr. Kemalo said that the herbs should be sought immediately to safeguard the animal's life. Ngila quickly went to look for the leaves, and she was summoned by the husband thus: "Be boiling water as I go to look for those leaves to save the mother of our family. If it dies, it will subject our lives to problems of buying milk because others cannot feed the family and their calves." Mr. Kemalo told them, "Cows are regarded as mothers of people. So they feed their young ones and people as well."

"My father taught me not to live in a home without livestock, especially a cow for milk. The wealth in the family is the cow and not any other goods because it gives milk and meat and brings wives home in the form of dowry. So I have them; they are riches," explained Mr. Kemalo. Mr. Gigali reappeared into the compound with a bundle of mumogu leaves contained in a bunch he had cut from the mother tree. The wife Ngila had boiled the water in a big sufuria. "Two litres are enough, Gigali," said Mr. Kemalo.

The water was boiled with the leaves and put in a gourd of about three litres. Villagers were asked to assist in holding the cow to make her drink the boiled managu leaves with water. The black cow was held by the head, and one old man advised them to put fingers into the nose to make it co-operative. Five people held it, and the water mixed with leaves was poured into its mouth in the prescribed quantity.

Mr. Gigali said it should be left to feed at home and asked his wife to supplement the food he had brought in the morning. He left for Ngemwe's home for the occasion. Ngila remained looking at the animal pitifully. Other cows were driven to graze in the field, and Ngila had taken the rope she usually used to carry loads and tied it loosely around the neck and later tied the other end against a tree stump in the compound. The cow could not feed. She collected leaves from the banana plantation behind the houses, but it would not taste or even attempt to feed.

Chapter Seven

Almost the entire day, the children remained seated next to it, calling its name, but it would not respond. Finally, Mr. Gigali reached Ngemwe's home at around 10.30 a.m. and met two old men who had already arrived and were waiting for others to arrive. He enquired for Ngemwe, who was discussing an issue with his wife behind the goats' pen. Mr. Gigali greeted the two old men in the Amakia council of elders' greetings because he knew they were group members. They responded in their respective language. *"Bareba haba wasundi*?" meaning, "How are you, members of Amakia council of elders?" "Bareba haba wee," responded the three elders.

He sat outside the main house with the three elders before he was called by Mr. Ngemwe to where they were standing with his wife. Mr. Gigali entered the main house with Ngemwe's wife, and the three men were invited into the main house after a few minutes. "Come in," said Mr. Gigali, beckoning with his right hand. They entered and were shown where to sit. Mr. Gigali went to where the honey beer was prepared and tasted it with a wooden cup. He took two sips and pronounced it mature. He asked Ngemwe's wife to hand him boiled water. He also asked for honey. He took boiled water and honey, mixed them together, and put them into the pot. He tasted the beer again and said, “It is up to the standard we required.”

Mr. Gigali washed his hands and removed some of the mulombe catalysts from the honey beer, which he put in one of the wooden trays placed next to the pot. He was called again by Ngewme's wife. "Mr. Gigali, please come," said Mrs. Ngemwe. He came out of the house and went in the direction the voice was coming from. "What do we do first, serve them with honey beer or tea I have prepared before others arrive?" asked Mrs. Ngemwe.

"We are taking tea before the others arrive," said Mr. Gigali. The other people did not hear the discussion because it was quite a good distance.

Mrs. Ngemwe entered the house where the old men were seated with cups in her hands. Gigali followed her with a jug of tea and a child behind him with roasted bananas. Ngemwe also came and took a seat in the same house. "I have locked away all the dogs for safety purposes; don't forget to feed them in the course of the occasion," said Mr. Ngemwe to his wife. Mrs. Ngemwe served the old men with tea and roasted bananas as they waited for other old men, advocates, and judges to arrive. Before Ngemwe sat, he greeted the elders by shaking their hands. And finally, he welcomed them to his home. They introduced themselves as misters Ngelo from the Amalu clan, Lomite from the ankire clan, and Jambana from Amugore clan. "Many more were coming who were summoned by your father, Mr. Tambalilo," said one of the old men, Mr. Jambana.

He told Mr. Ngemwe and his colleagues in the house that the case would be discussed by experts of the traditional culture who are members of the Amakia council of elders. He told them they would all be involved in the discussion. Ngemwe's father came accompanied by his wife, Sibero. Mr. Tambalilo entered the house and greeted the members of the Amakia council of elders in their language, and they responded in the same language. He greeted others with the usual greetings, and they also responded. Mrs. Tambalilo also entered, greeted everybody, looked around, and said to Tambalilo, "You have done the right thing to have summoned these 'Amakia council of elders' members from all the corners of the community the way you told me last evening. Master Tubelo is my husband; I slaughtered a big white he-goat for his mother; I visited that family the second time accompanied by my husband. Tambalilo, my elder daughter, Muribo, and two other relatives, Mr. Mberi and Kilambo, I paid for two goats, one goat, which was expectant, and a he-goat, the size of the one in our goats' shed. I cannot let my blood be taken by other people. The Amakia elders are hearing what I am saying," Sibero shouted loudly.

The husband, Mr. Tambalilo, said to his wife, “Leave the argument to the Amakia council of elders. You can brief them on all that you know about this matter. Still, you know that it can be subjected to rigorous and sensitive conditions affecting advocates and council of elders' lives and those of their generations and close relatives." The colleague elders were looking at Tambalilo. When Sibero heard those remarks, she kept quiet and left the house slowly and quietly, rubbing her hands in protest and disappointment. "Tubelo is my blood," she shouted as she left the room.

As she was leaving the house, she met with three other men coming in carrying their sitting stools, an official staff, and a blanket hanging on their shoulders. They were not able to move confidently and properly because of their age. "Good afternoon, mother of the people," the old men greeted Sibero. "Good afternoon, my sons," responded Sibero. That is how; the greeting went to people of different ages and from that community. The greetings of that community were according to age grade, age set, the relation of one person to another, fathers and sons and daughters.

All non-members of the Amakia council of elders were greeted in the same language or greetings by fellow members. The greetings for the members were reserved for members only, and nobody else was allowed to use them for greeting. If a member of the 'Amakia council of elders' was dismissed or interdicted on disciplinary or ethical grounds, he was not supposed to use the Amakia greetings until his interdiction or suspension was lifted.

The three old men who came were: Mr. Idambi from Athane clan, Mr. Jerile from Antumbane clan, and Kebu from Akame clan. Only one person did not come; he was Mr. Nemberi from the Mukare clan. The others, who had not reported so far, were Mrs. Ngemwe's brother Mr. Halore, Ngemwe's brother Mr. Murema and Mr. Lomete from the Amalu clan, who was a strong advocate, intelligent person but not a member of Amakia council of elders. A non-member of the Amakia council of elders may be listened to by the council of elders as a party but is not allowed to join a secret session to determine the ruling of the case as his views from him cannot determine the ruling.

The non-members, who are clever and intelligent, are referred to as good players who are not conversant with the game's rules in progress. Before they were served lunch, Mrs. Ngemwe's brother had already arrived but was talking with his sister-in-law near the chicken house. He came and greeted others in the ordinary language. All the members of the 'Amakia council of elders' knew that he was not initiated into the Amakia council of elders. He took his seat next to his brother-in-law.

Ngemwe called him, and they went outside to discuss something in privacy. Then after a few minutes, they invited their father and Mr. Gigali to their secret session. They later returned to the house to join others. They agreed that there was a quorum, and the discussion could start. Their father also told them that the honey beer could now be served after a few minutes. Only two elders were not taking honey beer: Mr. Jerile from Antubene clan and Mr. Nemberi from Mukare clan. Mr. Gigali said there was enough tea for them. He went outside and told one of the ladies, invited to serve the two elders with tea, to bring him one jug with sugary tea and the other with sugarless tea. That lady entered the house and passed the message to Mrs. Ngemwe. Mrs. Ngemwe was about to add sugar to the two sufurias she had prepared. When she was informed that with sugar in the wooden cup, she commented, "Omulili, I was about to commit a social crime!" She put the wooden cup down and asked them to repeat the instruction. They repeated, "Two jugs, one with sugary tea and the other one with sugarless tea."

She reduced the sugar in the wooden cup by half, put it into one of the sufuria, and asked one woman to stir for her as she looked for more cups because more elders had arrived in the main house. "They need to be seated before they wait to be served." When other women asked her how they knew those who took the beer and those who did not take beer, she responded that her father-in-law, his father, and Mr. Gigali could make out the difference so easily. "Mr. Gigali is popular among them, and he is their member in social places; therefore, when I take the cup, he will know who is taking what."

She left the tea preparation to another lady and opened another room where she kept utensils. There were utensils in that room, honey, and ripe bananas and eggs in crates which she collected from the chicken's house. She invited one lady to assist her in carrying the utensils and other required items from the store. They took all the required items from the store, and she closed it. She was assisted in removing the cups, plates, wooden spoons, and some three jugs and spoons. She carried the utensils in a wooden container.

She greeted those who had not been greeted previously and those absent when she entered the room. One of the old men, who had a bearded cheek and bald head, commented, "Sorry, Mabe, you look busy to cater for our social welfare and comfort; we shall shave and leave no hair on your head." "Thank my son," responded Mrs. Ngemwe.

Mr. Ngemwe and his brother Murema burst into laughter. However, the old man continued and said, "All the stones must be turned today, and no stone should remain in its original position."

Mr. Ngemwe and his brother Murema communicated with each other and said in low tones that only Mr. Lomette from the Amalu clan had not reported. Then, Mr. Murema called his father outside and framed the issue to him. Mr. Tambalilo told Mr. Murema, "Some things are minor in this case. Mr. Lomette is a single seed in a calabash that your mother fed you with. He is our numerical strength and not our professional expertise. We can do with or without him. The major source of our strength is the Amakia council of elders, who are present here. They have all come, and I am comfortable and confident. You should be able to tell how you know the child is yours without fearing because they will put any question they don't understand to you until you make them understand."

"You answer like a man, although you are not a member of the Amakia council of elders. Yours is to feed them with the true and right information. We inspected the child, Tubelo, with your mother, and he has most of our physical features. I checked and inspected the sexual organs; they are the same as ours- the fingers, the feet, the eyeballs, the ears, the mouth, and the head. Master Tubelo is our real blood, and even your mother confessed the same thing. Your mother also may be called by these elders to tell her story about Tubelo. Still, she won't be questioned because women are not taken seriously by the Amakia council of elders, which is from our ancestors' tradition.

But I know your mother has the facts the way she tells me and the way she inspected the child. She says the eyeballs belong to her, which I also confirm. You may not know, but we have confirmed this with your mother. She can take the baby by force if allowed because she says Mr. Adima and his family want to steal her blood and strength.

But if we do this, I can be heavily fined by the Amakia council of elders and looked at as a junior member of this council or considered at the level of non-members. So, we don't do something as council members for professional and ethical reasons," said Mr. Tambalilo to his son. "From now, we can start when we enter the house, and I will conduct introductions." He asked his son to enter the house and start the discussion before alcohol conquered their reasoning and consciousness. They feared that the strong honey beer might affect their behaviour, attitude, and sense of reasoning.

When they entered the house, all the people, who were there, kept quiet as if they were waiting for them. Finally, they all sat down like others, and then Mr. Tambalilo stood again almost immediately. "Let us pay attention to each other to enable us to fulfill what made us come here in my son's home. Mr. Ngemwe, I have my home in a separate compound, which is why I am saying 'his home'."

He asked Zeem Idambi from the Athiane clan to open with a word of prayer. Zeem Idambi started with a traditional prayer launching on the supreme being Munguku, and all the elders ended with a chorus 'enbele', the supreme being is great.

"Thank you, Mr. Idambi, for leading us with a word of prayer, and at this juncture, I would like to ask everybody to make an introduction, and this should touch on your name, from where in terms of clans, and whether you are a member of Amakia council of elders or a non-member. From there, I can go to the next chapter. Let us start with an elder to my left here." He pointed to his son Murema. Mr. Murema introduced himself as Mr. Murema, son of Tambalilo and a non-member of the Amakia council of elders. "No, you are not my son; when you are here, you are a public figure in your own personality. All you contribute is in your capacity as a member of the clan.

We started to part ways when I authorised your circumcision, and I married for you. All you say is independent Mr. Murema, a member of the Ankire clan," commented his father. Mr. Murema repeated and introduced himself the way he was corrected. All the people in the house made introductions, and Mr. Tambalilo introduced himself last and said he was the convener of the meeting. He told the people who had come that everybody had come to hear what they had called them for except Mr. Lomite, a non-member of the Amakia council of elders. He asked his sons whether they had received his apology, but they kept quiet as if they were unsure of his apology.

Mr. Tambalilo said that all people are explorers; the only difference is the distance and radius of exploration. All the people, who were there, could not know what he was saying, and they were free to listen. He said, "My son Ngemwe, who is living in a different compound, got circumcised about forty-two years ago and belongs to Litabe age grade. He explored this world, landed in the Antuambare clan, and came into contact with a lady named Urende, daughter of Mr. Verilo and Warimbo. He is said to have impregnated Urende, and she bore a son named Tubelo.

Another secret lover to Urende, Mr. Andima, was also claiming the child. I visited the baby when it was a week old and slaughtered a he-goat to its mother, Urende, with the cooperation of her family, and later, after one month, I paid for two goats. I bought them from Mberole market. One goat was four months pregnant, and a he-goat could be bartered with three miniature goats. Again, this was in cooperation with my in-laws to be."

Mr. Tambalilo sat down and thought that the best advice should be after consulting the Amakia council of elders, who are the custodians of traditional customs and culture. He told them that was why he had invited all the clans' spokesmen in the four communities as they had heard from the introductions.

"Zeem Kelu from Akame clan, you are the oldest and the most experienced in the tradition and culture of our community. You also told me one day that my grandfather was a great member of the Amakia council of elders. You are also ninety-six years old because you have told me that your mother Akale told you that you were born when the first white man came and danced with our great, great grandmother. He had a book preaching about Suye and his apostles. And from there, his brother came with a gun, conquered you, took your land, and made you his subjects. You also told me that your father paid money to the preacher's brother with a gun. You also told me your father went to seek employment on his farm to be able to pay him tax and left you with your mother, who was newly married to your father. Therefore, Zeem Kebu and other elders of Amakia council of elders, listen to the history of this matter and, if possible, save my son from losing his son to strangers," said Mr. Tambalilo.

Mr. Tambalilo added, "I am not Ngemwe, I am his father, and we are now members of the clan in the big sense. Mr. Ngemwe knows Urende better than me because he knows her nakedness better than anybody else before Tubelo was born and maybe even now. He is a grown-up who can explain himself better than anybody else. I know his mother more than their lovers. So he can explain to you the head and the tail of the story with his lover Urende and her son, Tubelo.

My grandfather, Andide, used to tell us that only the roof of the house can tell what lovers discuss at night. I, therefore, leave the ball on Ngemwe's court," ended Mr. Tambalilo. All the elders looked at Mr. Ngemwe. He was bending his head down and also intertwining his fingers. Mr. Jerile told him to update the council members on his lover's and the child's history. All the people in the house looked at Ngemwe. Mr. Jerile added to him, "It is only the lover who can tell the nakedness of the other one. This is what my grandfather Mandi told us when we were newly circumcised, but I could not interpret it, but today I put the answer while studying in the school of experience. Mr. Ngemwe, you have been studying in the school of experience with your lover, Urende. Enlighten us to be able to justify master Tubelo's identity as one of our sons both in Adami village and Amaki clan," said Mr. Jerile, as he pointed and faced Ngemwe squarely.

Mr. Ngemwe narrated how he met Urende as a young girl and how they came to love each other. He told them he used to sleep with her openly because he could stay in her house at night until the following day. He also told the elders that he was also engaged in assisting her father, Mr. Verilo, in his duties of grazing the cows and taking care of the animals left at home, especially the goats and calves.

Mr. Ngemwe told the elders that he developed friendship with her brothers Awendo, Bendebia, Chabalo, and Dakembu. He used to assist them in their garden. After two months while staying there, Urende told him that she was pregnant with him, and there was no quarrel because he had loved her for all that period.

He told them that he had informed his senior wife and his parents. And when the child was born, my mother, father, wife, and other relatives visited the child. After that, my father slaughtered a he-goat and paid the other goats to Urende's parents. Then, as I was preparing to bring Urende home, another man, Mr. Adima, claimed to be Master Tubelo's biological father, and I heard that he had paid part of the dowry. "And this is where the meat is plastering against the cooking pot," said Mr. Ngemwe. Mr. Ngemwe said that his grandfather used to educate them on meat plastering against the cooking pot.

All this time, Mr. Gigali served the elders beer and tea as they listened and discussed the issue. Another elder from the Mukare clan, Mr. Nemberi, asked whether there were other people to brief them before they discussed the matter because the issue was sinking into their ears. Mr. Tambalilo said that he had visited the child with his wife, Siberro, and maybe she could be listened to, although women are women in the world of men and the world we inherited from our ancestors. "That is true, but we can listen to her," said Mr. Kebu from the Akame clan.

Mr. Ngemwe went outside and called his mother, and she entered the house. The elders could hear steps in the direction of the house. They were seated discussing the issue. Sibero entered the house with her head scarf on her head. She was wearing a red dress and a black overcoat. Mr. Kebu started to ask Sibero, "Sibero, you are the mother of this household where we are seated today. Can we know from you the history of your said grandsons in a neighbouring clan and in dispute with Mr. Adima, the son of Meri?"

"I used to hear of such history when I was a girl at my home, Mbula, and before I was circumcised, but I couldn't believe it until I became a victim of circumstances. Some fourteen months ago, my son Ngemwe loved a girl by the name of Urende as his second wife, and I heard through his wife and his father that a son had been born after sixteen months of love. Of course, I was happy, and as usual, I spat on my chest to praise the creator of heaven and the earth who resides in the Nyarembe forest. I asked my husband to accompany me to see the child born and choose his name. I chose his name Tubelo meaning the one who wrestled others, because I heard Mr. Tambalilo was a wrestler in his youth and before he was circumcised. I did not stop there; I paid a he-goat to be slaughtered to my mother and followed that with two goats I was rearing in my house.

On all these occasions, we were together with my in-laws. When I passed there the other day, I saw the two goats, but they had increased to three because the pregnant goat gave birth to a male kid. When we were there, I checked and inspected the child from head to toe, which was indeed my blood. I tied a string on the right hand of master Tubelo to signify my grandchild among other people's children, but Miss Urende might not have known through her mother Warimbo or the father Verilo might have known it. I told Urende never to remove that string from his right hand until he steps into his clan where he belongs." So explained Sibaro with a lot of bitterness and spoke with high tones until she was asked to lower her tone. At times she shouted, "How do I speak in low tones when somebody is taking my blood to a strange land? I can sell all I have to fight this war before the Amakia council of elders and beyond." She was clapping her hands and making light jumps.

"Are you through, Ms. Sibero?" asked Tebi. "Yes, I am through. But until the conclusion is made on Wednesday in my favour, I am not through," added Sibero as she left the house, clapping and shouting as if there was a misunderstanding in the house. Her husband Tambalilo followed her and told her not to throw seeds at the birds, and she kept quiet and joined other women in the kitchen.

Everybody was satisfied with Ms. Sibero's explanation, which was marked as one of the ways to fight that war. Moreover, the elders had no doubt that the young Tubelo was Ms. Sibero's family member according to her birth history and the cooperation of both families.

Mr. Ngelo from the Amandu clan said, "According to Sibero's testimony, she had blindfolded the other parties to the extent of declaring ownership in broad daylight. The parents of Urende and Urende herself cannot run away from the testimony of Ms. Sibero. She has given testimony that will make us ask to be subjected to all Amakia council of elders' conditions to take the child if all that she has told us is true. The child belongs to Ms. Sibero's house and is a member of this family and clan." All other elders concurred with Ngelo. "Sibero had an intelligent, clever, and informed mentor in her seclusion," added Mr. Ngelo. "That is a wonderful plan she architected all alone," added Mr. Lambano from the Amugene clan.

Chapter Eight

Mr. Gigali added more honey beer to their calabashes and wooden cups. "She remained with a child almost the whole afternoon, and I did not know what she was doing, nor did she tell me," said the husband, Mr. Tambalilo. "We have all the reasons to stick to Mrs. Tambalilo's evidence and testimony," said Mr. Ngelo. He also said that they wait and hear from another party. Mr. Ngemwe called Mr. Ngelo outside for a discussion between the two, where Mr. Ngemwe wanted to know whether they should send for Mr. Lomente from the Ankire clan because there was a need to do so, and it was a very effective method. Mr. Ngelo told him unless he wanted him to meet them, enjoy his honey beer or add to mechanical strength. "We have all the Amakia council members we wanted, and Mr. Lomete is one of them," responded Mr. Ngelo. "A dog without teeth to bite is useless to its owner but may be spared for other uses. My father always told us this and told us not only to bark but to bite," added Mr. Ngelo.

He told them when we approach the elders of the other party, who are members of the Amakia council of elders; many of us would be surprised by the professional terminologies which would be used and the language which may not be understood by some of us. Non-members like you will only listen and relate your experience in your mother's tongue. They will discuss the issue in the Amakia council of elders' language using professional terms in the presentation of the case. And before the case is concluded, the selected elders will take a secret session at a distance and decide the case. Many of us may not be present in a case of this nature. Our party will include only two elders: Mr. Tambalilo from the Amugane clan and Mr. Jerile from the Antumbane clan. Others would be listeners and contributors who would wait for the verdict of the elders.

He told Ngemwe that to be a non-member of the Amakia council of elders is a loss and a discredit to him as an individual and his relatives, and the community at large. One cannot be able to help himself from a sensitive issue like this one or save any other person in the clan or the community. That is why; they refer to non-numbers as numerals meaning they are there when it comes to issues before them as a figure because one is not qualified for any positive contribution to the issue in question. "Your father may not have told you, but you are a liability to the family where you are born, to the village, and to the clan of Amukire," added Mr. Ngelo. "So, be a member to protect yourself and others regarding such issues. You are a man because I can see that you have property, but that property can be destroyed by them because they have the ability and platform to do so," added Mr. Ngelo to Ngemwe. He told Ngemwe that his father, Mr. Tambalilo, was a prominent elder in both the village and the clan, and that was why he invited them, and they responded. "Others may invite us, and we don't respond because we don't see the reason for coming. We were not coming to take your honey beer, but we were coming to save a situation invited by the other elder. That was why; he withdrew when he explained his position and left you to brief the elders on your position. He cannot say for you because you are not a child. A child can be protected together with women but not a man who is mature to be a member like you," concluded Mr. Ngelo.

Mr. Ngemwe told Mr. Ngelo the position of the matter. They both agreed and entered the house for more discussion on the matter, which would be discussed the following Wednesday by all elders from the clans constituting the community. Five wooden jugs were standing on the ground and were full of honey beer to be taken by the elders. Mrs. Tambalilo came to the house where the elders were seated and discussed and asked whether they needed more of her input. The elders told her that what she had told them was enough, and now they were on the part of the lovers themselves, and when she asked that, she quickly commented, "I withdraw my comment," and then left the house quickly to join other women in the compound.

Mr. Adambi from the Athane clan wanted to know whether there were more issues for discussion. Mr. Nembari from the Miakare clan and Mr. Ngelo from the Amalu clan said that they had nothing left un-discussed in their personal capacities. But Mr. Ngelo said that his grandfather Mwarelo, who had died twenty-five years earlier, told him not to conclude a public issue unless they asked him to do so. "Don't say I am the final person to do or say this or that," said Ngelo. "Others are there to speak their mind," added Mr. Ngelo. "That is the position," other elders looked at one another as if there was no more material. Mr. Kebu, from the Ankame clan, asked other elders to speak their minds to save time and open their mouths for the honey beer because their mouths were half-open because of the important issue, which was to be discussed and concluded. He asked the elders to compile what they would capitalise on the material day.

"We have heard enough from all the parties, especially Mr. and Mrs. Tambalilo, who are the parents of Mr. Ngemwe. We have also heard from the mouth of Ngemwe himself, who is the victim and, in the language of the white people, 'the horse's mouth'. We are sure that the story we have gathered from these people is almost enough, if not enough, to enable us to compile enough evidence, but this is after hearing from the other party. My father Mubari used to tell me not to conclude the case from one party, and I agree with what he told me because this was from the experience he gathered in his life. He also advised me to be a good listener than a commentator. I also conceived that idea. So I am saying that when we get to Avembe chief's camp ground, the case venue, let us report early for a consultation to know our opponents. Let us also be careful about the chief's elders who would listen to the case under their chairman Mr. Mwandame. He has a big role to play in that case. There are seven chief elders, including the chairman, Mr. Mwandame. If possible, we can approach Mwandame through his wife Odesi, who comes from my clan; we know each other. And that is all I have for the day and my conclusion," concluded Mr. Kebu.

Mr. Ngemwe's brother-in-law Mr. Mindebe wanted to know where they would meet before the case started and the time for commencing the case. Mr. Kibu told him the chief elders' case would usually start at 10.00 a.m., when all parties were expected to have arrived. He also informed him that they should all meet at the chief's camp compound in the Avembe chief's campground because they came from different clans in the community.

The fees were also discussed at the meeting, and Ngemwe's father, Mr. Tambalilo, paid the fees for the case, which would cost one thousand Dibari, and the winning party would pay another five hundred Dibari. "There are other expenses to be incurred," said Mr. Ngemwe. "There is transport for all these elders and advocates," said Ngemwe. He counted ten people to be transported from their homes and back. There would also be meals for that day.

"Do we need to meet the chief of Avembe location before the case, or do we do without him?" asked Mr. Kebu. "The chief, Mr. Binidu has all this information and knows the ruling but cannot reveal it to anyone," added Mr. Rebu.

Mr. Tambalilo said, “The chief is an important figure in the area he represents and should be told what is happening even if the answer is obvious. He may interpret that we are overlooking him,” said Mr. Tambalilo. “Let us send somebody to tell him with something whether we are looking for a favour or not,” added Tambalilo.

They all agreed that the chief should be told with three hundred Dibari. Mr. Ngelo was appointed to do it that night or the following day in the morning. "I will trace where he will reside today, either at the first wife's home or in the second wife's home, before I go to sleep for the night," said Mr. Ngelo to his colleagues. That day, several relatives had come to listen to Ngemwe's case and make a material contribution to supplement what he had.

There were Ngemwe's sisters, Mrs. Malebu, who married in the Athane clan, and Muribo, who was older than Ngemwe and married in the Antuamba clan. They had contributed two thousand Dibari to Ngemwe's case to be held the following Wednesday.

The elder sister Munila was accompanied by her two sons Master Alibe and master Birole, who had been newly circumcised the previous month. Mr. Ngemwe had given each a goat before circumcision. There was also Ngemwe's youngest sister Tolebi who was also the last born in the family and was living with the mother and had brought two big cocks.

His brother Murema had donated all that was used on occasion and would donate another similar amount to feed the elders and advocates on that Wednesday. All the arrangements for Wednesday were well-programmed, and Mr. Murema, the brother, was left to coordinate everything until the last day. After that, Ngemwe was allowed to rest and listen to the case and the outcome. Mr. Tambalilo, his father, was assigned a job to make all the payments, including meals for Wednesday and transport for that day and Wednesday.

It was also proposed and agreed that the honey beer should be prepared around Avembe chief's camp compound for the elders and advocates to take after the case. And those who did not take alcohol should be given sixty Dibari each.

They took the honey beer but could not even drink half the pot because of the alcoholic concentration of the beer and how it was prepared by Mr. Gigali, an expert in preparing that kind of honey beer. Mr. Ngemwe told the sisters, other relatives, and friends to take the beer in small wooden containers and take it to their husbands at home and other people in the households. Ms. Sibero was very happy to see her married daughters coming to support Ngemwe in the battle of master Tubelo who wanted to be taken away by a stranger. "I can't afford to see a stranger taking my blood to his home; I can use all that I have been looking for in life," Mrs. Tambalilo snarled. "Tubelo must be here to graze my animals," she added. The elders sprayed honey in the compound to bless the family. They were comfortable with the drinks and food they took that day and the welcome by family members.

They left the home of Mr. Ngemwe at 4.30 p.m. They were escorted to the gate by Mr. Ngemwe, his brother, and their father, who had invited them for his son and as a member of the Amakia council of elders. They left for their homes to prepare for Wednesday, the day of the great case over the possession of a child in dispute of the biological father, which would be determined by a council of elders together with the mother, Ms. Urende.

She was invited as a major party to the case. On their way home, all the elders were happy with Mr. Tambalilo for preparing a good occasion for them. He had also slaughtered a he-goat where they were served with meat and soup to dilute the honey beer they had taken for about four hours. They discussed the case as they walked to their respective homes. Before they separated, they all agreed that the father of Urende would take responsibility for that dispute because there were procedures laid down by the Amakia council of elders safeguarding marriage. If he was a council member, he could be heavily fined by the council by paying a 'forty-five' fine to the council and return all the dowry and other payments to the losing party. If not, he could be interdicted with immediate effect. The elders went home waiting for the great case to be held on Wednesday before the chief's court at Avembe chief's camp. Mr. Tambalilo spent the whole of Tuesday at his son's home to see that all the arrangements for Wednesday's case were in good order. He ensured all money for payments to the elders and advocates was there. There was money for court fees, meals for elders and advocates were present, and money to pay after the case. He also ensured that the honey beer was prepared early in the morning around the Avembe chief's camp to be taken by the elders after the case because the elders and others would be thirsty.

Mr. Gigali had left early in the morning with three other people. One lady was carrying a pot, the other person was carrying honey in a small tin, and the other one was to stay at the place where beer was prepared for the night until the honey beer was taken and prepared the items used in the preparation back home. Mr. Ngemwe had sold one of his he-goats to sponsor the case. The he-goat he sold had fetched three thousand five hundred Dibari at the local market. His wife predicted that if the he-goat was sold during the season of the plenty, it would have fetched about six thousand dibari. But since the occasion demanded, it was okay.

Ngemwe's wife was prepared to attend to the case at Avembe chief's campground, accompanied by Mr. Ngemwe's sister Muribo who was older than Mr. Ngemwe. Mrs. Tambalilo was prepared to leave early in the morning before everybody else left. She said she would prepare breakfast before the cock crows, serve Tambalilo and then leave for Avembe chief's ground to wait for the case to start.

"This is a serious matter affecting my immediate family and keeps me awake at night and disturbed during the daytime. I will rest when Tubelo is here, with or without the mother. I will work the formula out using my food crops in the store and in the garden; I don't want any other project from today on," Mrs. Tambalilo said before her clansmen and relatives. Mrs. Ngemwe and her mother were washing the clothes and preparing other things for the following day's case. Mrs. Tambalilo was seen at the homestead, then after a few hours on Ngemwe's compound with her daughter-in-law. She could send her daughter-in-law to her home to wait for her. They were packing as if they were taking a long safari to a distant place. Washed clothes were drying on the cloth line in Ngemwe's and her mother's homestead. People saw them washing in the morning and drying on the line during the day.

Mr. Tambalilo was seen going in the direction of the Ankire clan, which is in the Avembe location, around 5:00 o'clock in the morning, accompanied by his son-in-law from the Amugane clan, who was wearing a white shirt, black shoes, and a navy green coat. When Tambalilo arrived at Avembe location, he looked for Gigali and found him in the home of an old friend Mr. Sambero. He had prepared honey beer in a big pot and was now adding honey. "Where did you get the mulombe catalyst?" Mr. Tambalilo asked Mr. Gigali. "I borrowed from my friends here who were my age mates when we were young boys before circumcision," responded Mr. Gigali.

“Mr. Gigali, when can it be mature?” He responded that it would be mature by 10.00 a.m. of that day. So, there had to be somebody to add more honey around midnight to make sure it would be ready by morning. He tasted the pre-mature honey beer and pronounced it concentrated. Then, Mr. Gigali took green banana leaves, covered the pot, and tied a string around the neck of the pot. The owner of the home met Mr. Tambalilo with Gigali and greeted them. "Good evening, my fathers," Mr. Sambero greeted. "Good evening, my son," he responded. After greetings,

Mr. Gigali introduced them to one another and explained why they had prepared the drink at the place. He told him that was not bad because they were from a distance, and there was nothing else they could have done.

"People are interdependent. My father used to tell me no man can shave his hair unless he is shaved by another," said Mr. Sambero to Mr. Tambalilo. Then, they organised how the honey beer would be taken the following day and whether it would risk security and the chief's representatives. Mr. Sambero assured them there would be no problems as long as the honey beer was not for sale and noise levels were minimised.

Mr. Sambero asked Mr. Gigali to see one of the headman's representatives and inform him that there would not be any problem if the headman's representative was aware. They made arrangements to meet the headman's representative that evening, and Mr. Sambero said that he would assist in looking for the headman's representatives and seeing that the situation was contained. He asked Mr. Gigali to accompany him to meet the chief representative in the market near his home.

They proceeded to the Umero market and started looking for Mr. Mandevu, the chief's representative in that area. They looked for him and were able to trace him after three hours. They met him talking to another representative of the chief from another sub-location. The chief's representative knew there was something that Mr. Sambero had for him, but he did not know the other man with Mr. Sambero, his subject in the sub-location. They greeted the chief's representative, Mr. Mandevu, and he asked them to wait for a little so that he could finish with the other man he was talking to. When they finished talking for a while, he came to Mr. Mandevu and greeted them again. "How are you, Mr. Sambero, with your friend?" he greeted and asked them why they wanted to see him. They replied, "We are fine, Mr. Mandevu." They looked for a place to sit and discuss what they had gone to meet him for. Mr. Gigali explained. Mr. Mandevu replied, "I know the case of Mr. Ngemwe and Mr. Adima over a child ownership that is born out of marriage by their lover Urende. That is the case," said Mr. Gigali.

Chapter Eight

Mr. Gigali, Mr. Sambero, and Mr. Mandevu proceeded to a building where there was a restaurant and sat to discuss. Mr. Gigali paid sixty Dibari to Mr. Mandevu for his transport home. "Be careful, don't make noise while taking your drink, and don't invite many people from this area. Be alone and take quietly, and don't sing as you take the drink," advised Mr. Mandevu, the chief's representative in the respective area. "We shall take your advice seriously," said Mr. Gigali. Mr. Gigali and Mr. Sambero then wished Mr. Mandevu goodbye and left. However, Mr. Gigali had prepared to stay there until the following day. He even learned that the chief was aware of the case through Mr. Mwandame, the chief's representative and chairman of the chief's court.

The chief knew of the case, and when the struggle started some months ago, the chief had launched investigations over that case from various sources, including the lovers and Ms. Urende, the daughter of Verilo. The case was well-established, and the chief's elders knew the answer. The Amakia council of elders are the elders listening to the case and, simultaneously, ruling over the case. However, the case must be listened to for all the parties to prove their facts and arguments before the chief's court elders, who are conversant with the traditional law of the land and are well-experienced in that area.

Mr. Sambero and Mr. Gigali, on their way to Mr. Sambero's home, passed through a place with a bar and stopped to take one for the road. They stopped at a bar with the words "*On the Way Home,*" written at the top. They met other people there, and it was at around 5.00 p.m. They took a separate table in the bar where there were no customers around where they sat, and Mr. Gigali called the waiter to where they were seated. The waiter came, and Mr. Gigali asked Mr. Mandevu to ask for his choice of the drink he preferred. They ordered two beers, and the waiter left them to go and bring the drinks. They talked as they waited for the waiter to come with their drinks. Finally, Mr. Mandevu revealed to Mr. Gigali that they should present this case well and without fear.

The other party might decide not to come because they already knew the case's outcome. But he told Gigali not to make it public or tell the plaintiff. He should wait for the elders to make a ruling on the case. He pleaded with Mr. Gigali not to betray him to his colleagues. "Give them a lot of courage to present the case well," said Mr. Sambero. The waiter came carrying two beers as they had ordered. "Can I get a clean calabash?" asked Mr. Gigali. "Bring two of them," added Mr. Sambero. The waiter looked around when he heard the voice of Mr. Sambero. He indicated with his two fingers, and the waiter understood the language Mr. Sambero was talking.

He returned with two calabashes of equal size, which were clean and properly washed and dried in the sun. "Here is a government personnel who comes to inspect this house every day. He inspects the cleanliness of the bar and the utensils used in the bar. The drinking utensils are properly inspected, and he advises the bar owners to wash with hot water and dry them in the hot sun. So, we feel comfortable with the utensils and the government person. If the bar owner doesn't follow the instructions, he asks us to make an immediate arrest, and that's what we do, and take you to the police who further take you to the court of law," said Mr. Sambero to Mr. Gigali.

He told Mr. Gigali that the chief was not only concerned with security but also those whose children did not attend the white man's school. They would be fined in court, and those who were not having toilets were also fined. Another serious thing was criminal activity and cleanliness in the eating places. The chief's representatives were many, and if anybody brought trouble, especially fighting in the bar, he could be arrested immediately and locked in the chief's cell to be taken to the police station the following day. On top of that, he was taught law and discipline.

They took beer up to 7.30 p.m., and then they departed to Sambero's home, where a place was prepared for the night. Sambero's wife welcomed them and served a meal for both of them. "This is my old friend Mr. Gigali, the owner of that pot I told you about yesterday. They will be here with his colleague from the chief's court on their way home," said Mr. Sambero. She greeted Gigali and introduced herself as Mrs. Sambero or Mrami.

"Thank you, Madam," responded Mr. Gigali. The meal consisted of cassava, boiled bananas, green vegetables, green peas, and chicken soup. They were given hot water to wash their hands and a towel to dry their hands. They washed and wiped their hands dry, and Mr. Gigali thanked her again for her service, and she responded, 'Adem'. 'Adem' in their language meant 'come again'.

They took supper, and since they were a bit drunk, Mr. Gigali was shown a place to sleep near the pot of honey beer. He told Mr. Sambero that he would wake up to check the maturity of the beer and add more honey at night, and he was assured of security and freedom in that home. The home was far away from the main road and was well-fenced with very strong wooden poles and shrubs fixed with nails. The compound was well-fenced. The house, where he was shown a place to sleep, was the next room to where the pot was kept. The other two people in that building were housed there. The building was about forty feet long.

It was far from the owners' house, which was a hundred feet apart, and each had its own compound. In the building where he was housed was a permanent gate that was secured with a padlock and could not be seen from outside. There were dogs in the main compound where the owner was housed. Mr. Gigali was assured of security at night. The toilets were fifty feet away from the house where he slept, but he was assured of even going out at night. He was provided with a torch and a *panga*.

The people in that building told Mr. Gigali that there were no wild animals or criminals such as thieves in their area. If anybody was caught stealing, the chances of being burnt to ashes using dry banana leaves or taken to the police station half dead were very high. Therefore, the people had become good citizens of that place. If the chief suspected a person of being a criminal, he would order the arrest using the representatives in that area. They arrest you immediately and take you before the chief. After an interview, one may be taken to the police station.

Mr. Gigali had been shown a room with a wooden bed and a mattress with two blankets - One to spread on the bed and the other to cover himself. A fireplace with fire also acted as the lamp to light the house. There was firewood in the house to keep the fire burning if he wanted. He was also given a key to the room where the honey beer was maturing. At around midnight, Mr.

Gigali awoke to check on the honey beer. He removed the green banana leaves and tasted a little with a calabash. He took fresh honey and added it into the pot when it was mixed with hot water. Next, he removed some Mulombe catalysts and put them out from the pot to a calabash which was next to the pot.

He covered the pot with green banana leaves and tied the pot with a string to avoid entering a foreign body. Then, Mr. Gigali used his torch to close the house and entered his sleeping room. His neighbours in the other rooms were coughing to alert him that they were aware of his movement from that room to the other one and that there was nothing to fear. He was also happy to learn that he had security from those others around him. Finally, he returned to his sleeping room and added firewood to the fire because it was becoming cold in the room.

Chapter Nine

On Wednesday, the day of the case, Mr. Sambero woke up at six to take care of his animals around his compound. He had prepared the animals together with the food they would use for that day. He had prepared the goats, milked his cows and gave them food, and stored the other food for the day. He had also provided food to the chicken and collected the eggs laid the previous day. He opened the main gate, entered the compound where Gigali slept, and knocked at his door. "My friend, my friend," called Mr. Sambero. "Yes, Sambero," he responded immediately. He opened the room where he slept and greeted Sambero, who was standing at his door. He invited him for breakfast in his house. Mr. Gigali followed him. He had not prepared his bed when he woke up.

They entered the main house, and Gigali was asked to have a seat. Tea was prepared that morning on the table, along with roasted bananas, yams, and five boiled eggs on a brown calabash. Mrs. Sambero opened the bedroom door and appeared in the table room. She greeted Gigali and asked them to prepare for morning prayers. She said the prayers before taking breakfast and welcomed them to the table. They were served with tea by the wife, and before she served Mr. Gigali with tea, she asked him whether he preferred hot millet gruel, and since Mr. Gigali did not respond, she served him with tea. The husband took gruel from a calabash, tea, and roasted bananas, and then he took two boiled eggs.

They took breakfast, and then Gigali asked him to go with him to inspect the pot. When they arrived at the compound that early morning, the people were awake and were preparing to go out to attend to their businesses. They entered the room where the pot was kept, and Mr. Gigali untied the rope that secured the pot and removed the green banana leaves that had covered it. When Mr. Sambero realised there were no calabashes to serve, he brought three calabashes from his house, one of which was meant to serve from the pot and fill the others. He filled Sambero's calabash. "We don't drink in the morning; the authority has restricted people from drinking in the morning hours until noon hours. Morning hours have been reserved for work. If you are not working, you are not allowed to drink during those hours. But I can taste," Mr. Sambero said.

"This honey beer is one of the strongest that I have tasted," said Sambero. He took one calabash and refused to take another one. "I am also a leader assisting the headman in executing his duties, and that is why we do our work in the morning and leave my wife to do the rest," said Mr. Sambero. He left Mr. Gigali behind to take care of his colleagues who were coming for the case.

Mr. Sambero took time to discuss with his friend Gigali before he left for the headman's meeting at the camp. Before he left, he ensured his animals, including the goats and chickens, were well-fed. He also went around his fence and compound to ensure that nothing strange had occurred during the night. Mr. Gigali requested him to be allocated more calabashes, and he asked how many, in addition to the three, they required. Mr. Gigali said they could use another twelve. Mr. Sambero went to his house and asked his wife, Mrami, to assist with the number of calabashes that would be returned in the afternoon. She went to her store, took twelve calabashes, and asked her husband to take them to his friend.

Mr. Sambero told Mr. Gigali to wash them after use and leave them with the workman at his compound. Mrami would be waiting for them. Then, he left for his commitment at 8.00 a.m. and wished him and his colleague success in the case. Before he left, he told him to keep his secret until the secret was unfolded. "Don't speak to please anyone, but the truth of the matter is as I told you," said Mr. Sambero at the gate as he left. "You shall remember me later for what I told you about the case. Do not tell them that I told you. Rumour spreads and spoils the first party," added Mr. Sambero.

Mr. Gigali thanked Mr. Sambero for accommodating him in his home and letting them together, along with other colleagues, hold the party in his compound. In addition, he thanked him for having revealed to him the answer to their problems, which had brought them there. Mr. Sambero left and wished them success in their endeavour. The day had already unfolded, and the people had started using its light before darkness could come. There was light everywhere. Clouds had not completely disappeared from their positions on the earth.

On the eastern side, where the sun rises, red light could be seen from far. People were streaming on the way to attend to their daily businesses. Some were alone, some walked in groups to keep each other company, and some walked together as a group. There was green everywhere because they had planted crops some thirty days earlier. Mr. Gigali was met by Mr. Ngelo, who was accompanied by two other people he had not seen before, Mr. Adake and Mr. Luzi from the Amalu and the Akane clan, respectively, who were distant relatives of Mr. Ngemwe.

They had official staff carried by the Amakia council of elders, only for identification purposes when they were listening to the case which concerned them and the case they were handling. They knocked at the compound's gate, where Gigali was preparing the honey beer and arranging the utensils. There was another person who was sharing the same building with Gigali that night and had not identified himself to Mr. Gigali before. He opened for them and asked for Mr. Gigali. They entered. He told them that he had not known of that name around and didn't know him, but Mr. Gigali had heard when they were discussing and went outside to receive them. "Here he is," shouted Mr. Ngelo.

"I did not know him, and he is a stranger here. I only met him last night and knew that the compound's owner knows him well," said the man who had opened the gate. They greeted Mr. Gigali and were shown where to sit on a log in the compound under a Mututia tree. They rolled the log to where there was sunshine because they wanted to enjoy the warmth of the morning sun. "How was the night at Avembe location, and how do the birds sound from here?" asked Mr. Ngelo. "It is the same as our home, but the security here is a different one because there are many security personnel under the chief and recruited by him, and criminal activities are minimal, and that is the major factor in the development of a place and subject in general," said Mr. Gigali as he welcomed them.

Mr. Ngelo had been sent by Mr. Tambalilo to come, inspect, and know where the elders and advocates would rest after the case. Mr. Gigali summoned Mr. Ngelo into the room where there was a honey beer pot and took the green banana leaves off the pot. The honey beer was making sounds as if it was alive. He was given a calabash cup and took a little to taste. "This is strong beer and can affect us against the case we shall be presenting before the chief's court, the elders, and advocates. If we take it carelessly, we can mess with the case and leave the court compound as defects," said Mr. Ngelo. Then, he called his colleagues who had accompanied him, Mr. Turubi and Mr. Ndibo, each of whom was given a little to taste. Also, he said that the beer might mislead them in the case if taken in an unspecified quantity according to its alcoholic content.

Each of them was given a quarter of a calabash which they had approved to take to have their normal sense while handling the case. Mr. Gigali informed them that beer was not allowed to be taken in that area up to noon hours. Since the place was not authorised by the government as a bar, they should take the beer without making a lot of noise and not be accompanied by anybody from that area. "The compound owners, Mr. Sambero, had served me with the instructions before he left. He also advised me to pass the information to you that the case should be thoroughly prepared. Facts should be presented by tough Amakia elders who are well-prepared, intelligent, and experienced in our people's traditional customs and culture.

The chief's court has very tough elders appointed based on their membership of Amakia council of elders' institution and experience, and well-educated in the traditional laws," stated Gigali. Mr. Ngelo responded and told him they had strong, experienced, and talented judges and advocates, who were initiated into the Amakia institution seventy years ago, and have been having elders and advocates for sixty years. He added that even the chief's elders would recognise and know them when they arrived. "They are about to come because they left our village at around 5.30 a.m. They are encumbered by age in walking quickly and for long distances. The other elders are escorting them because they cannot be left behind," said Mr. Gigali. He filled one of the calabashes and gave it to his neighbour in the compound. Before the neighbour took it, he told him, "We don't eat or take any drink before the owner tastes it." Mr. Gigali tasted and swallowed the honey beer. He took the calabash with yellow liquid and commented, "Thank you, my friend."

Mr. Gigali told him they were coming with other colleagues after the case at the chief's camp compound at Avembe to take the drink.

"You are welcome," the man said.

The four walked outside the compound and left for Avembe Chief's camp. They joined others on the way. Some were carrying Amakia elders' official staff, and the three men, including Mr. Ngelo, greeted in the language of the Amakia council of elders. But, Mr. Gigali was excluded from the greetings and was not part of the greeting because he was not a member. They went together towards the chief's camp where the main road proceeded to Amma market and beyond. Mr. Ngelo understood that they would present and hear various cases at the chief's court. He interrogated them and understood that two of them would present and assist Mr. Adima, Mr. Ngemu's respondent. Mr. Ngelo told them he was proceeding to the same venue to listen to a case.

As they moved, they joined people on the way, some with Amakia elders' official staff and others without. There were also bald men with grey hair signifying their age and others without grey hair but were aged too. Finally, they arrived at Avembe chief's camp. The gate to the camp was opened, and there were people either standing or sitting in groups. The people were still coming and filling the compound. Mr. Ngemwe and his colleague entered the compound and stood to look for his other colleagues who were coming with him.

He saw Mr. Nemberi from the Mukare clan standing, accompanied by Mr. Idhambi from the Athane clan, beside a Mumbege tree. He, together with other colleagues, went in their direction. When they were about to get to where they were standing, Mr. Idambi saw them and said, "Our people have arrived." There were two greetings when they joined Mr. Idambi and Mr. Nemburi, one for Amakia elders for its members and the other, the ordinary greetings for Mr. Gigali. Then, they settled and discussed the contents of the case.

"Where are the others?" asked Gigali. "I am asking because I spent the night here to take care of the drink after the case, and all is taken care of," said Gigali. Mr. Gigali told them that he was surprised by the security situation in the area, which harbours no fear even if one is a stranger in the Avembe location. "Even if you walk at night here, the only thing you will be required to do is to identify yourself and say where you are living or going and what you are doing or going to do and where.

They may escort you to where you are going for confirmation purposes. And if you are known as a criminal, they can pick you even in a place like this before the people and lock you in that room," said Mr. Idambi as he pointed at the room beside the chief's office. "You are guarded by the chief's representatives until the next day when the chief interrogates you, and then you are released or taken to the police station for further action. If the chief is not present, the chairman of the elders can also free you or order to take you to the police station," added Mr. Idambi. "The chief's court chairman Mr. Mwandame, also the chairman of the court cases, is a very important person in the Avembe location and in this compound. He almost has the powers of the chief and is not employed by the government. The residents respect him a lot, including me, for settlement of issues and security matters here," said Mr. Idambi. He further told them that all cases with their facts must take their normal shape when ruled. He told them that apart from that, he was intelligent, honest, an experienced elder, and never entertained consultation through the back door.

Mr. Mwandime always said in broad daylight, "Nobody should take what doesn't belong to him or her, including justice in this court." While referring to the chief's court, Mr. Mwandame was a respected person by both the chief and his subjects. The majority of the cases had raised complaints, and some, which had been appealed in other institutions coming from another chief's court, had stood the ruling of the chief's court. So, many people had confidence and faith in the chief's court under the membership of the chief's court elders and the chairmanship of Mr. Mwandame.

As they were discussing, Jerille from the Antumbani clan and Mr. Kebu from the Akare clan, Mr. Jambaro from the Amugare clan, accompanied by Mr. Lomett from the Ankire clan, were entering the gate of the chief's camp. There was an incident in the compound, which had started a few minutes earlier, accompanied by Muumu from the crowd gathered in the compound. The crowd had noticed the presence of Mr. Jerille and Mr. Jambaro, who were the ruling elders, and advocates in the entire Mambe community and beyond.

Mr. Jambaro was carrying his official staff and a flywhisk while another young person was carrying his four-legged stool. The murmuring continued, and Mr. Ngelo asked, "What is strange with the crowd and the compound?" Then, they started looking around the compound. Most people were looking toward the gate, from where Mr. Jambaro was coming. Mr. Ngelo, who had headed towards the gate, saw Mr. Jambaro accompanied by his grandson master Mwandubi, his namesake. Mwandubi was an age grade that Mr. Jambaro belonged to and graded in his circumcision seventy years ago.

Mr. Ngelo met Mr. Jambaro and greeted him in the Amakia elders' language. "Bariba zeem Jambaro." "Bariba, Zeem Ngelo," responded Zeem Jambaro. "I am exhausted. My namesake woke me up at 5.10 a.m., as I had instructed him to do. Then, he prepared a fire in my house and woke his mother to prepare us. I then took my flywhisk and the elders' official staff and asked him to take my four-legged stool, and we left to this place at around 5.30 a.m., and here we are," said Zeem Jambaro, holding his grandson's right hand.

Many of the people in the compound had gone to see him. But those elders and other people, who knew him, said, "He has come." "He is regarded as the most experienced, intelligent, informed, and conversant elder regarding this land's traditional customs and culture. However, other elders fear and respect him because his words are taken as final when the elders and prominent ones leave for the secret session," said one of the chief's court elders.

Mr. Ndambalo, one of the chief's court elders, approached Zeem Jambaro and said, "Come, I'll lead you to a seat." He led him to the place where he was supposed to sit and helped him take his seat. Before he took the seat, he asked, "Where is Mwandubi?" Mwandubi was standing next to him with his four-legged stool, and before he finished asking, Mwandubi had held his right hand to give him the stool. "Place it in a good place where I cannot shake or fall," Zeem Jambaro advised his grandson.

Mr. Ndambalo took the four-legged stool from Mwandubi, placed it on level ground, and then asked Zeem Jambaro to sit. Zeem Jambaro lowered his goat-skin-bag on the left side, adjusted it to the right-hand side, and opened it. He took out three ripe bananas and looked in the direction of Mwandubi. "Take these bananas and eat them," he said while handing him the bananas. Master Mwandubi wanted to take the official staff from his grandfather as he sat. But his grandfather told him, "This is a symbol of authority as an Amakia council elder and not a walking stick or supporting stick as you take it, but I can support myself with it. I will educate you more about the stick when we get back home. I brought you here to escort me, observe how we shall be seated, the parties and their contributions, chief's court elders, the chairperson of chief's elders, and observe carefully. Then, when we go for the secret session where I am a member, you can follow us, but you stay at a distance where you can't hear our discussion," Zeem Jambaro told his grandson.

Before the case started, all the fellow colleagues in his party had come to greet him, and he asked them to keep around Master Mwandubi. "When you feel hungry, come and tag my back quietly and get your meal, I have it in my bag," said Zeem Jambaro to his grandson.

Zeem Jambaro took the small, black wooden container from his elder's bag, opened it, poured snuff onto his hand, and then closed it again. He then fed the two streams of his nose. Finally, he returned the wooden container back to his handbag and closed the handbag, then started sharing the discussion with other elders before the case started.

People, who were in the compound, rumoured that the case was about to start because the chairperson had come and entered the chief's office. However, the chief's court elders were around, and only three of them could not be traced.

The chief's court elders, who were present, were Mr. Heburi from Amalu and Mr. Pendero from Akame. Mr. Okimburi was preparing the place where cases are held, assisted by three other people. All the people felt the presence of the chairperson of the chief's council and court when the preparation of the venue began. People could be seen entering the chief's office and coming out after a while, affirming that the chairperson of the court was there.

Chapter Ten

The chief's camp compound was almost full of people who were parties to cases, their advocates, elders, and those who had come to watch for their friends and relatives.

At 8.58 a.m., Mr. Queme from the Ankire clan, Mr. Rindi from Amugane, and Mr. Sindalu from the Mukare clan were seen entering the compound, and all of them were carrying black official staff. The cases were about to start because the chief's court elders were all present. They entered the chief's office, and after a while, the others were seen entering the chief's office. Many suspected they were consulting before the cases could start.

The chief's court elders came from the office led by Mr. Heburi, Mr. Niabaro, Mr. Rindi, and others, and the chairman came last. He talked to the representatives who were guarding the cell and gave them some money. And one of the representatives opened the cell, and six people came out and were told to bask in the sun around the compound for three hours. They were instructed not to mix with people, but they could be seen by their relatives and friends, not in a group but one person at a time, and they should be thirty steps away.

One of the chief's representatives had indicated the boundary of thirty steps from where they were seated to bask in the sun. Mr. Mwandame had instructed the representatives guarding the cell that anyone giving food should properly identify himself or herself before the representatives. The person who was visited must be reported to the chief or himself. He also told the inmates that if they wanted to be released, they should confirm that they would appear to the Amakia Council of elders and confess that they would not repeat the same crime again through their parents and close relatives, who would inform the chief's court chairman or the chief after the cases were finalised.

One of the inmates Mr. Adabi, who was reported to have stolen a goat with its kid, pleaded through his father, who went to meet Mr. Chebiro of Amugane and a prominent 'Amakia council of elders' member and agreed to pay three goats to the owner of the stolen goat and another small goat to represent the kid.

Before the case started, the father of Mr. Adabi had brought the goats through an Amakia elder and was directed to make the confessions within three days, at his cost, to the council of elders and report to the chief's office on the fourth day. Failure to do that, he would lose the goat and be taken to the police station. He was then released, and the owner of the stolen goats took his goats home. All the residents were happy with the justice offered at the chief's office, including the court.

Before the chairman started the cases, all the parties were called and lined up according to how the case would start, and if there was a postponement, the parties had to be there so the postponing party would pay the postponement fee of five hundred Dibari. The elders and advocates of the two parties must be present, together with the plaintiff and the respondent. When the court chairman appeared, all the people looked in his direction; they were as silent as the rocks on the grassless and treeless mountain.

He entered through the way made by the crowd and got to his seat next to his second in command, Mr. Sindalu, who also commanded respect and was one of the subjects of Avembe and his colleague, the chief's court elders. All the people clapped and ululated when he entered through the crowd, and there were murmurs everywhere. They were not to do that for anybody, but they did it out of respect and love for him. When he came to his seat, he greeted the people, "Vulembi Omandu Avembi," while waving with both hands. The people responded, "Alambi chamave koti," in a thunderous sound and ululation everywhere.

He sat down and consulted Mr. Shindalu, who whispered to him in the ear. The chairman could be seen nodding his head in agreement. The people were also murmuring in appreciation of his presence.

All the parties were asked to be ready to answer and present their sentiments; if not ready to start the case, pay postponement fees. Mr. Okimbwi was the secretary, although the cases were not recorded anywhere. He was in charge of arranging and calling parties to the cases and the nature of the case. He started with the first case, whose plaintiff was Mr. Amande and the respondent was Mr. Buruka, both from the Mukare clan, alleged to have bewitched his child, master Chapedi who had passed away a month earlier on a Wednesday at midnight. "Mr. Mwandame, my advocate Mr. Dambuli is sick, and I, therefore, request a postponement until he recovers," said Mr. Buruka. "Please address the chair well. In this case, he is the chairman of the court and not Mr. Mwandame. Let us be official; I am also forced by office capacity to address him as the chairman. Can we stick to that, Mr. Buruka?" asked Mr. Okimbwi. "When will your advocate be well and okay?" asked Mr. Okimbwi. Mr. Buruka asked for two weeks and two weeks from that Wednesday fell on a Friday according to the program of the chief's court. Nevertheless, he went forward holding the five hundred Dibari and handed it to the treasurer, Mr. Queme, who confirmed to the secretary that he had received the money and could continue with another party.

Mr. Okimbwi called Mr. Dalo, the plaintiff, and Mr. Eliako, the respondent, who came from Amalu and Athane, respectively. The dispute was that there was a heifer under Amakia tradition transaction under questionable circumstances. Mr. Dalo, the complainant, asked for an excuse because his in-law had lost his child due to an accident in a flooded river while crossing from school in the evening. "Omla," said the secretary. He asked when they were due to complete mourning, and he said the mourning period would take about two weeks. "Do we also fix your case on Friday as the other one and on the same day?" asked the secretary.

"Yes, Mr. Secretary," responded Mr. Dalo.

The complainant of the other case was Mr. Elaku against Mr. Emakalu from the Amakia and Akame clans, respectively. The dispute arose from extending a land boundary at the Akame clan in the Mungari area. Mr. Emakalu also asked for a postponement because his relative, who had given him that land, had left to meet his uncle, who had a wedding for his daughter. He said he was ready to part with five hundred Dibari, and if possible, he would be ready that Friday. "What are the views of the other party?" asked the secretary. "Most obliged, Mr. Chairman," responded Mr. Emakalu. He was asked to square with the treasurer standing next to him. He counted the money in coins and handed it over to the treasurer.

The complainant, in this case, was Mr. Gale, who was cheated by his brothers when they divided the property of his late father, Mr. Halore. As a result, he inherited a piece of land that amounted to only two acres, while the other three brothers got ten acres each. He also complained that the bride price of the young sister was supposed to be his, but his elder brother Mr. Ibale had also cheated him out of that. "Don't say your brothers; mention their names for clarity," directed the chairman. He said his brothers' names were Mr. Ibado, the firstborn, Mr. Jambe, and Mr. Kefadi. The chairman nodded and said, "They are one party against you. Who is a party they should pay a responding fee of one thousand Dibari as you have paid? If the case is postponed, they pay five hundred Dibari each," said the chairman. Mr. Ibado was seen to hold his chin when the chairman spoke of payment for each brother if the case was postponed. He wanted to postpone because his paternal uncle, Mr. Kalemi, was away for official duties and worked in a public office.

"Mr. Chairman, my paternal uncle, is not available; give me a month to trace him. He is a government officer in the Teru region. I cannot confirm when he will be available, but I will do my best. So give me a month," he said. Mr. Okimbwi, the secretary, could be seen counting his fingers and gave him a Monday after thirty days from that day. "I am comfortable, Mr. Chairman; talk to the treasurer in your individual capacity," said the chairman. "I hope you understand what the chairman means when he says individual capacity," said the treasurer. He had summoned his three brothers and contributed the one thousand five hundred Dibari. He handed the money to the treasurer, which was in note form.

"To save time for others, all cases, which are for postponement, should go to a separate place to get the date and pay postponement fee as other cases continue," directed the chairman. "Or are you about to finish?" asked the chairman. "We have just four cases left, Mr. Chairman," responded the secretary.

The secretary advised the parties involved in the cases to agree on the date before they were called. "We have other cases to listen to and arbitrate today before the sun goes to sleep," added the secretary.

The other case was between Mr. Adalo, the plaintiff, and Mr. Maloka from the Athane and Amalu clans. The case was about breaching the barter of a bull and he-goat agreement made in August of the previous year. Mr. Maloka was not present because he had an urgent call from his son in Purimma regional headquarters where he worked as a doctor. He had sent his brother Nebundi to represent him. The parties had agreed their case to be fixed after the weeks that fell on Friday, fourteen days from that day. He further paid postponement fees, and they left the compound after consultation with the other party and their respective advocates and elders.

Chapter Eleven

The postponement of the cases took two hours to settle the matter and fix the respective dates and comments by the court's chairman.

There were few people in the Avambe chief's camp compound; most of them had come to postpone their cases because of unavoidable inconveniences caused by one of the parties in the respective case. Therefore, the chief's court was to postpone them against the postponement fees of five hundred Dibari. The chief's court chairman looked at the sun and said, "This is lunch hour, but we cannot break for lunch to keep this old man Zeem Jambaro here and leave late for his home with his grandchild who carries his four-legged stool. At the same time, he has not prepared to spend the night outside his house," said the chief.

The chief asked the secretary to check whether all parties were ready and present for the case to start. Mr. Okimbwi called Mr. Ngemwe and Mr. Adima to check on their elders and advocates. He also asked them to check whether Ms. Urende was present with the child, Mr. Tubelo, and the father, Mr. Verilo. Brothers of Urende could either be there but not necessarily as long as the father was present.

Unfortunately, Ms. Urende left when the child started crying uncontrollably. People could not believe it because she sat beside the gate under a Mungari shade. Nevertheless, many people, who knew her, went to greet her.

Mrs. Tambalilo tried to look for her in all corners of the compound. Finally, after looking for Urende without success for the case to start, Mrs. Tambalilo commented, "This is a bad omen; I got tripped twice on my left foot, and I suspected something bad ahead would happen to me. This is it," she said, angrily and continued, "Urende has taken my husband back to her father's home, and we were prepared to take master Tubelo, today using our facts, intelligence, social experience, economic power and other factors that favoured me," she said loudly and angrily.

The chairman of the court, his deputy, and the secretary of the court went into session for consultation. He agreed that the case could not continue without the mother of the child in dispute, who knew the answer to the dispute more than any other person. Therefore, they agreed to take the postponement fee from both parties. The next date was not fixed because Urende was a party on her own, and she needed to agree on the date fixed. The chairman asked the chief's representatives from every clan where the parties came from to take three dates with the break of a week. If they agreed on one common date, it should then be communicated to the secretary immediately for the summoning of the parties.

The two parties paid a listening fee of one thousand Dibari and five hundred Dibari for postponement. The chairman also directed them to pay a postponement fee of two hundred and fifty each for Urende, their lover.

Mr. Ngemwe wanted to pay the whole five hundred dibari for Urende. But the chairman refused and said, "We don't know who will win the child together with the mother or one of them. This will be determined by the elders who will listen to the issues in question and arbitrate accordingly," said the chairman. "So, you two are hanging on the elders," added the chairman.

All the parties were called together so the chairman could communicate the decision. He asked the parties to be comfortable until the issue was sorted out. He said, "In a case, there must always be the loser and the winner, so be prepared for one of the two." Everybody, especially the parties, had left the court compound. The chief was left with the court elders and those in the chief's cells. Their parents and relatives had come with the agreed fines accompanied by the aggrieved party and the Amakia council of elders' father, who would communicate to the chief's office the confirmation of confession before the council of elders by the victim.

Many goats in the chief's compound had been brought as fines. All of them had ropes on their neck to avoid escape. There were twenty-seven goats and seven cows. There were several groups in the compound. There was a group composed of the owners of the property stolen: the father of the thief or relative of the thief, 'Amakia council of elders' member, and the fine, which attracted the interest of another animal to remind the victims of that discipline in future.

Those not claimed by their parents and relatives were to be taken to the police station and then to the court, where they would be declared guilty or innocent by the magistrate in charge. The elders and advocates of Ngemwe had left for Sambero's home except for Zeem Jambaro and his grandson, who left for home immediately after the case was postponed to an unknown date. A honey drink was prepared for the elders after the case. Mrs. Tambalilo left for home in shock and was negatively affected by the state of matters she experienced when the case did not take off. She left the compound, clapping her hands in disgust.

She opened the gate on the left, which was unusual since she was married in that home. The workman, who was employed by her in her home, read her mood and took it as if she had lost the case. It was because she could not tell people what had happened with the case. She was not able to concentrate on her duties at home that evening. She even asked the workman to let the calves loose to suck because she could not be able to milk. The calves sucked for about fifty seconds before she asked the workman to lock the calves in their pen for the night. She could be heard banging utensils in the house.

Her close neighbours came to ask her how the case had turned out, and she told them that she had no mouth to tell what happened or what did not happen.

Those, who came to know of the result of the case, were left in surprise and made the wrong impression and notion of her. She kept the people in the dark about the matter. When the husband returned in the evening before 7.00 p.m., he briefed those who inquired and told them that the case would be heard later. The husband called the worker and asked him if he had eaten because he knew his wife would not cook. He asked him to wash the utensils and prepare the fire in his house. He made tea and shared it with the workman.

He asked the workman to get mature green banana fruits in the plot next to the compound and prepare them for roasting, which they did and ate as supper together with the bit of milk he had got from the cattle which had its calf dead. Those elders, who had left for Sambero's home, had enjoyed themselves with honey beer which had matured in the morning session. Mr. Sambero met them at around 2.30 p.m. They had followed his instruction as he had briefed Mr. Gigali. They were drinking quietly, and they had not invited any local person who would let out the secret to the chief or his representatives. When he arrived at his compound, he met them, drinking quietly. "Where is Gigali?" asked Mr. Sambero. "I am here," shouted Mr. Gigali. "You have made good arrangements while drinking. Nobody knows you are here, and nobody can suspect that there are strangers or beer in my compound because of your good conduct," said Mr. Sambero to Gigali.

"How was the case?" asked Mr. Sambero. "The case did not take off because the mother of the child and lover of the gentleman was not there, and only she had the answer to the problem we wanted to solve," answered Mr. Gigali. Mr. Gigali asked Mr. Sambero to be seated and take a drink. "There is a lot of beer, and the beer is a strong one which we cannot take much. Sit and take beer; you have assisted us to be here and enabled us to carry out our duties. May I call the owner of the case, Mr. Ngemwe, to come and greet you," said Mr. Gigali. Mr. Ngemwe came, and the introduction was done. "This is Mr. Ngemwe, who had the case in the chief's court, and this is Mr. Sambero, the owner of the compound where we are seated today, where I spent last night preparing this drink for you," said Mr. Gigali. They greeted each other joyfully.

"Sit, enjoy with us and take a beer. You can invite one or two of your friends to drink with us. We have enough to drink for today may be until some late hours. You have done wonders for my family," said Ngemwe. Mr. Sambero was afraid that Mr. Gigali had let the cat out of the bag, but he had not. Mr. Sambero invited two of his friends who came to accompany his friends at home. One was Mr. Wamugi and the other Mr. Amanduli.

When Gigali met them standing, he first greeted them, directed them where to sit, and quickly went to the pot. Then, he took a small gourd brought by Mr. Sambero, filled it with honey beer, and took it to them. "May I introduce my friends to you before they settle? This is Mr. Wamugi, my friend and brother in circumcision, who passed on the circumcision knife to me holding his shoulder with his right hand, and the other one with him, is Mr. Amanduli, the chairman of the youth who maintains security in this village. He is a man we respect because no insecurity is experienced in this village when he is on the committee," said Mr. Sambero.

Mr. Gigali welcomed them where they were seated, and Mr. Sambero went to his living house to get more calabashes because they were becoming fewer than the people there. Mr. Sambero asked his friends to take the beer sparingly because it would conquer their conscious. However, he asked them to be free in his house because there were enough rooms to sleep, and his wife could take care of their stomachs if they promised they would be ready to spend the night there.

"Thank you, Mr. Sambero; my wife is newly married; she moved into my home last two months and cannot stay alone in the house. Therefore, I will take one and then leave because I do not want to introduce drunkenness in our early married life, although I drink. I have never discussed drunkenness with her in our life as lovers, including now," said Mr. Amanduli, who did not want to take two calabashes of the honey beer.

He drank quickly and left. There was a lot of beer left in the gourd they were given. Mr. Gigali asked Mr. Sambero to get some to take to his wife, to which he replied, "Marero does not share a room with beer, leave alone taking it. Even her children are not allowed to touch anything associated with taking beer. She even tells me not to send children for utensils to take beer or collect them from the beer storage, and that is why I am going to take them myself because I cannot ask them to bring them to me," said Mr. Sambero. He had also promised to take one and half calabash and asked Mr. Wamugi to take the rest.

Wamugi also said the beer was strong as if it was prepared all week long, and even seasoned drinkers could not take four calabashes. He took two calabashes and asked his friend Sambero to escort him to the public road and then disappear towards his home.

The elders and the advocates were still taking the honey beer at Mr. Sambero's home but slowly. They did not allow themselves to get drunk because they felt the effect of the beer and the distance they would travel from the place they were drinking. Mr. Idambi told the advocates and elders to drink the beer carefully because they would cover a considerable distance by foot. They all agreed.

Mr. Jerille reminded Mr. Tebu and Mr. Nemburi that they should know that they would walk a longer distance than the rest when they reached their land, and he, therefore, asked them to take beer and leave in time. Mr. Jerille again reminded them that his grandfather told them that the sun does not wait for a judge, and he did not explain the meaning.

Mr. Nemburi told the elders that he had only registered to reach home that day, and time was running out. Mr. Nemburi told his colleagues, "We have spent the day well, but it was spoilt by Urende in the eleventh hour." All the elders and advocates, who had come to present the case, blamed Urende for the black day she had turned to them. "Let us not discuss that issue anymore; she may be one of us and forget all this," said Mr. Ngelo. They said the topic should be stopped because it made Mrs. Tambalilo mad whenever she was reminded of the child, Master Tubelo, the subject of the dispute. She felt uncomfortable when reminded of all she had paid to claim the mother and the child.

"Happiness at times turns into bitterness," said Mr. Tebu. This is what Tebu was told by his father when they were grazing livestock during the day. Mr. Tebu told them that Mrs. Tambalilo's happiness had turned into sorrow, which should not be that way because the case had not been touched. "We had potential to win the case, and even the rival party and others in the court knew that until the whole situation was frustrated by Urende," said Mr. Tebu angrily. Mr. Ngelo reminded them they had agreed to close that topic until they got home. Mr. Nemburi reminded them to leave that topic alone. "My grandfather Akike used to tell us that the wall has ears; can we also respect the ears of the walls by leaving that topic?" said Mr. Nemburi as he took a sip at his beer.

The people had come to report a case of stealing to Mr. Sambero, and Mr. Gigali asked Mr. Sambero to invite them in for a calabash of beer because they were about to leave and some beer was still left in the pot. The two came and sat next to Mr. Sambero, seated on a trunk cut from the mother tree using an axe. It was placed on the ground. Mr. Sambero again went into his living room and brought along two calabashes to serve Mr. Mbale and Mr. Soneti. "I have also been invited by these friends here who had prepared the beer in my home," said Mr. Sambero. They were served with beer in a gourd, which was half-full. Mr. Gigali then took the two empty calabashes and filled the calabashes held by each of them in their hands. He kept the gourd down and asked them to serve themselves whenever they finished. Mr. Sambero commented, "Thank you, Mr. Gigali, that generosity is enough; they can serve themselves; the ball is now in their court." Mr. Gigali went to manage the beer pot and the people and arrange how they would return to their homes with his colleagues. It was also getting late and hours to return home beckoned.

Mr. Nemburi kept his calabash down, which was half-full, and said, "My father told me that time does not wait for a judge, so we are no exception." They all listened without sipping.

Mr. Tebu stood and went where he could see the sun and said, "True, we may be late for home." They all looked at the sun, which was setting to the west, and rays were striking them through the leaves of banana plants and trees where they were seated in a group. They changed their drinking style and agreed that what they had taken was enough; if it was not enough, they must stop there. Mr. Gigali consulted Mr. Sambero because of the utensils and other items used for the occasion and the balance of beer in the pot. They agreed on how the pot would be transported home in two or three days.

Before they prepared to leave, only a little beer was left in the pot. Mr. Gigali told his host, "Can you assist me in keeping the Mulombe catalyst in the sun to dry and avoid spoiling?" "Obviously, I should be able to do that," responded Mr. Sambero. Mr. Gigali consulted Mr. Sambero, and they all gathered behind the building where the beer was prepared and where Mr. Gigali had spent the night. Mr. Gigali introduced Mr. Sambero for the second time and said he was an old friend when they were younger. He thanked him together with his wife, who was opposed to alcohol but had allowed it to be prepared in her home.

He asked one of the elders to say something, and Mr. Jerille addressed them, expressing gratitude for the generosity they had received from Sambero's family and especially his wife, Marero, to have allowed them to prepare beer in her homestead.

Mr. Jerille added that their objective was obstructed by the nuclear of the case. He had become impatient before they came to his home for refreshment and the good reception they received from Sambero's family. He concluded with thanks. Mr. Sambero, in return, thanked Mr. Gigali for his generosity because all his friends, who had come to meet him at his home, did not leave the compound without getting a full calabash of honey beer and obeyed the instructions he gave him.

He also thanked Mr. Gigali's companion for talking and discussing in low tones to avoid attracting attention from the chief and his agents. "You have not betrayed me by your presence here, and I am happy. You are welcome in my home until you finalise the case with the chief's court," they were thanked and commended by Mr. Sambero. They all thanked him in unison and dispersed. They also bade goodbye to Mr. Mbale and Mr. Sonet.

Mr. Sambero reminded the elders to take all the paraphernalia they brought, especially the elders' official staff. "Thanks, Mr. Sambero," said Mr. Nembura. "I had forgotten mine where I was seated." So he went and collected his official staff. When another elder, Mr. Idambi, inspected his snuff gourd from his old man's handbag, it was missing, and he started looking around for it. He went where he was urinating and traced it behind the fence and on top of dry kuumu leaves. All the other elders started to inspect themselves, and they had no shortage of anything they had brought into Sambero's compound. Mr. Gigali dipped his hands into his pocket and took out one hundred Dibari, which he gave to Mr. Sambero and asked him to take it to Mrs. Marero to buy soap to wash her calabashes and other utensils used on occasion. Mr. Sambero took the money and thanked Mr. Gigali on behalf of his wife. "Women are simple and appreciative. She will be happy and share the occasion with you," said Mr. Sambero. Mr. Sambero escorted his visitors to the main gate, which boarders his land with the main road. They thanked and shook each other's hands and wished each other goodbye.

Mr. Murenge expressed the sincerity of the host and the hospitality he had shown and told them that he was one of the few good people one can encounter. They unanimously agreed with Mr. Murenge's sentiments about Sambero. Mr. Gigali quickly led them towards their home, and some of the elders even lagged behind. Mr. Tebu disapproved of Mr. Gigali's speed and said, "Young man, do you think my mother, your mother, and the mothers of these elders became pregnant the same night?" "Why, Mr. Tebu?" asked Gigali. Mr. Gigali stopped to answer the question, and all the elders arrived where Tebu was standing to answer Gigali's question.

"Why do you push us with that speed? Slow your pace and be patient; we are not women who gave birth the other day and thus are rushing to suckle the children," said Mr. Tebu. Mr. Lomete also agreed with Mr. Tebu that they were going far, but they should not get home exhausted because of both speed and distance. Mr. Gigali said that he was used to walking quickly since childhood but would adjust and walk at his colleagues' pace. He started taking shorter strides for the older men to keep up.

"I can breathe now," said Mr. Tebu. When he completed saying that, all the elders laughed, including Mr. Gigali. "My mother told me that I was born when the first people were sold by the traditional chiefs here; the men dressed like women, who had beards and sticks breathing out fire," said Mr. Tebu.

Everybody laughed again in unison when they heard of men dressed like women with sticks breathing out fire. Mr. Tebu asked, "Are you laughing, and is that my history from my mother's mouth?" Mr. Idambi said it was long ago and added that the chiefs, who sold and traded with people as their goods in the market, were cursed by the remnants of the community they sold and that almost their entire family had become extinct.

"The remaining family members can be counted, and everyone knows them in this community and tribe," added Mr.

Tebu. "The traditional chiefs made a lot of wealth from the trade of people. They also turned to use hunters who collected ivory and took it to them, and then they would sell it together with the people to supplement their business," Mr. Tebu told his colleagues.

Mr. Gigali wondered how people were sold and how much each person was worth. Mr. Jerille also told them that his grandfather told them about traditional chiefs or leaders who sold the subjects they disliked and those who were disobedient. They would be tied with ropes and chains to avoid escape. The area where people live today had depopulated because of greedy traditional leaders who were out to make wealth. Mr. Jerille told them that one of his relatives was sold and has never been traced to date. He told them his father told him that when he was still a boy. He added that the traders were using other goods for exchange against people, and some chiefs were given sticks that breathed out fire. The chiefs were also trained on how to use those magical sticks.

Chapter Twelve

Mr. Gigali had, by now, slowed down to their pace.

They walked and passed Mulime ranges, and after a little distance, they crossed river Muraru, which bordered Avembe and their home sub-location. Mr. Nemburi told Mr. Gigali that his grandfather Muvandi told him that anything already started has an end, but anything not started has no end. He continued and told them that once the journey home was started, it must have an end, and if they stayed at Sambero's home, there would not be an end to the journey. They walked for one and half hours before reaching a crossroads, and Mr. Nemburi asked those taking different routes to wish others goodbye. Mr. Nemburi and Mr. Kibu took the route leading to the North, Mr. Jevulle and Idambi took the southern route, and Mr. Lomete, Mr. Ugelo, and Mr. Gigali took the western route.

Mr. Ngemwe took the south-western route alone, but other people were traveling on that route. Women were coming from their crop plantation, children who were taking their livestock home, and men and women coming from the marketplace with logs and other big loads on their backs. After walking a short distance, Ngemwe was joined by two neighbours who were coming from Kirinendia market to buy a he-goat which had been demanded by Amakia Council of elders to clear themselves from witchcraft administration and practice. They tried to know from Ngemwe the outcome of the case, but he told them the case had not been concluded by the elders because of some logistics which had arisen.

They also told Ngemwe that their case had been fixed for the following week, on Friday. Therefore, they were preparing and collecting elders from all the clans for consultation before that day arrived. Ngemwe told them if the problem was cleansing themselves with a he-goat, there was no need for many elders because the case was already concluded. “But, Mr. Ngemwe, one has to confess at the sacred groove before the elders in your support; otherwise, opponent elders may administer to you the wrong or harmful oath, and we are non-members of Amakia council of elders,” said one of Ngemwe’s neighbours, Mr. Kabende.

Mr. Ngemwe agreed with them but told them there were elders before entering the sacred groove. "Sacred groove is a blessing to some parties in dispute and curse to other parties," he responded.

Mr. Kabendi said he had a lot of faith in the chair of the court, Mr. Mwandame. He explained to Ngemwe that if he had the truth and presented it before the elders, they would listen to his arguments and facts well. But Mr. Kabendi told Ngemwe to have members of the Amakia council of elders who are experienced with the tradition and culture of the people. Mr. Ngemwe was told that the elders must also be good presenters of the case and intelligent in the presentation because they use some professional language you cannot understand, but they understand your presentation.

“How are Zeem Jambaro and other elders in that case?” asked Ngemwe. "Is he one of the elder advocates for your cases?" asked Mr. Kabendi. "You have a strong elder if facts are there, and you present them well and intelligently," said Mr. Kabendi to Mr. Ngemwe and his colleague Mr. Mwendaro. “The court elders respect Mr. Jambaro’s uprightness, experience, and conduct as a member of Amakia Council and moral conduct as a member of the council,” said Mr. Kabendi. “Thank you,” thanked Mr. Ngemwe. Mr. Mandaro was pulling a black he-goat behind him. They proceeded to their homes as they discussed issues related to the cases. Mr. Ngemwe wanted to know the goat's price, and Mr. Kabendi told him they had bought it at three thousand eight hundred Dibari after a lengthy bargain. The initial price was four thousand five hundred Dibari. Mr. Mandaro said that the seller had completely refused the money until they had been forced to put it back in their pockets.

“This is the only goat in the livestock market enclosure, which satisfied the required standard we were directed by the elders of the council," said Mr. Mandaro to Ngemwe. When Mr. Ngemwe explained the particulars of his case to Mr. Mundaro and Mr. Kabendi, Mr. Mundaro said, "Your case is technical because of the other party; you are likely to take an oath in the sacred groove." Mr. Ngemwe tried to know why he had to take the oath in the sacred groove. Mr. Mundaro told him their case was technical and complex but would unfold when presented to the court elders. "If there are objections from the two parties, that is a straightforward case to the sacred groove. However, the party, which will be granted the he-goat oath, is doubtful to me as a non-member of Amakia Council of elders," added Mr. Mundaro.

Mr. Mundaro asked Mr. Ngemwe to ask his God to help avoid the sacred groove. "That area is not the best for us young people," said Mr. Ngemwe. "But your father is allowed to take the oath on behalf of the family," said Mr. Kabendi. Mr. Ngemwe said he did not want to be associated with oathing in the sacred groove. Mr. Kabendi told Mr. Ngemwe that he was personally opposed to the oathing in the sacred groove but had been forced by circumstances.

"My grandfather Dimo used to say that when one is alive, he is a friend of problems, and when one dies and becomes a member of the other world, the problems disappear from him," Mr. Kabendi told Ngemwe. After walking a short distance, Ngemwe branched to his home, and the other two proceeded to their homes, a distance of about a kilometre to the south. Mr. Ngemwe bid them goodbye and branched to his home, which was about a two-minute walk from the main road.

When he reached his compound gate, Mr. Ngemwe knocked at the gate and called out, "Who is here? Who is here to open the gate for me?" Mrs. Ngemwe came to open the gate with her leso tied around her waist. The leso was reaching almost to the ground. When she got near the gate, she asked who it was, and he said, "I am the chief of this location, and you are my deputy who takes over the office if the boss is not present." She opened the gate and just looked at him. She knew how he behaved when drunk and when sober. She closed the gate and followed Ngemwe to his house, where he resided and kept the goats.

He opened his house and went in. The wife went to her house on the heath and took fire to light him a fire. She lit the fire. The goats were busy consuming the leaves brought a few hours ago. He went and dropped onto his bed. She went to her house and brought food.

She tried to wake him up, but he was too tired and drunk to wake up. Finally, she woke him up and gave him food in a calabash she usually served him in. He took several spoonfuls, placed the food beside the bed, and locked the house for the night. Before the wife left the house, she reminded him to close the house from the inside. She came to check whether the house was closed and shook the door to know whether it was well-closed. She confirmed and left for her house to feed the young children before they left for bed.

He slept comfortably in his house, and within a few minutes, he had started snoring loudly, audible from a few metres from the house. The wife went round to see whether all the animals they had kept were in good condition and whether their enclosures were properly kept and closed to avoid straying into the compound at night, especially when he was drunk. When the pigs noticed her presence, they made a lot of noise as if they had not been fed that day. She went round all the places animals were kept. She visited the goats' place, cows' pen, pigsty, and chicken building to ensure they were properly locked for the night. She prepared the beds for her children and ensured they slept well in their respective beds. She was now comfortable with the compound and rested in bed around 9.30 p.m. because she had prepared dinner early.

The compound was quiet without the noise of any living thing. He could not get any more sleep after four hours of sleep. He could not stay in bed until morning. He could no longer close his eyes and therefore had to sit on the bed because there was nobody to light a fire for him. He did not want to wake his wife because he knew she had taken a lot of trouble throughout the day to prepare the animals and feed them with the family. He went out to pee, and the wife heard and called his name. "What are you doing outside at this hour of the night?" She asked. "I cannot close my eyes and therefore forced myself to come outside and breathe some fresh air," said Ngemwe.

She went outside and lit the fire on his heath. He told her he wanted fire but was uncomfortable calling her at night to light the fire for him. Mrs. Ngemwe knew her husband was tired from the day's exercise and walking to and from Avembe chief's camp. Mrs. Ngemwe knew her husband had not eaten the food she had kept in his house. She showed him the food, and Ngemwe took it in that state.

"I will take the food as it is because I don t want any noise at night from utensils. I also don't want light in my compound at night," said Ngewme to his wife. He then told his wife that their grandmother told them when a person lit a fire in the heart of the night; he invited spirits into the home. So they entered through any hole in the house, no matter how small and hid somewhere where the owner of the house could not know or imagine. "That is why people come, cook, and sleep, and there are some who put out the fire to avoid lighting at night," said Ngemwe.

She was escorted by the husband to her house and was scared by Ngemwe's story told to him by the grandmother Tobeto. Ngemwe took her to her house and went inside to ensure there were no spirits as told in the story. She locked her house tightly, and then went back to bed. He was left to nurse his tiredness and the state of drunkenness from the honey beer they had had the previous day, Wednesday. He kept reflecting on the previous day's engagement, especially the interruption they experienced from Urende and the resources they wasted for that day. Finally, he went into bed to rest and was unable to sleep. He stayed awake until morning when other people woke up and started engaging in their daily businesses.

That Thursday, when the day broke, he woke up very early at 5.00 a.m. and started preparing his animals. He went to the nearby bush and brought leaves for his goats; he entered his banana plantation and got the banana trunks for his cows, gave food to his chicken from the store, fed his pigs, and cleaned their houses. At 6.30a.m., he could be seen preparing the compound where the cows and sheep, which graze in the field, could feed. He was also seen collecting the remains of the previous food and throwing them into the banana plantation. He was busy that morning and did not want to remember the last day's happenings.

Mrs. Ngemwe came to milk the cows and met them well-fed that morning, including the tethered goats and sheep. She had no problem in milking because the cows had been fed. She milked the cows and went into her house to prepare tea for the family. By the time tea was ready, the children had already woken up. She had also roasted bananas for her husband, who liked taking them during breakfast. Within a few minutes, tea was ready, and the wife was serving her family.

She half-filled the jug for him and took it to him together with roasted bananas and three boiled eggs. She entered his house and kept the meal on an improvised table. She came out of the house and looked for him in the compound without success. She later saw him coming from the direction of the toilet. "The breakfast is ready in your room," she told him. "Thank you," responded Ngemwe as he approached his house. When he entered his house, there was tea in a jug placed on the table, roasted bananas from a banana breed that he liked eating, and three eggs in a calabash.

Ngemwe sat in a locally made chair and started taking his breakfast. As he took breakfast, he reflected on the previous day, which was wasted by Urende, and no useful work was done to develop the family's economic welfare. He blamed Urende for the wastage. As he took breakfast, he programmed the day's work. He had taken care of all the animals in the compound. The previous week he had spent two days on the banana plantation. The only place, which was not prepared well, was the crop plantation which was taken as women's work. He checked his left pocket and had little money left. He checked under the banana barks mattress, took his black bag, three hundred Dibari, and put them into his pocket.

He went out of his house and called his wife. He was holding a panga, ready to start the day. The wife responded, and he asked her whether she had completed preparing the plot, and she said there was a small portion left on the upper side of the plot at Murendure. So he gave the three hundred Dibari to her and asked her to get some people to complete it that day or the following day. Mrs. Ngemwe took the money and went to her house. He then headed for the gate.

The fence around the gate had grown into a bush, and he started to shorten the cropping plants growing towards the household compound. First, he sharpened the panga on the sharpening stone. Next, he cut the creeping plants and those that had overgrown the required level all around the entire perimeter.

This took almost half a day's work. Finally, at around 9.00a.m., he sensed that the panga was losing its sharpness and went back to the sharpening stone to sharpen it again. When he returned, he started where he had left and went round cutting. After an hour, Mr. Gigali met him. “How did you spend the night, Mr. Ngemwe?” asked Mr. Gigali. “It was fine, Mr. Gigali, and you?” asked Ngemwe, "I spent it well; I got home at 8.00p.m., and all was well together with my animals,” said Gigali.

"I thank all my colleagues who had come for my assistance. You also managed the occasion very well, and I am happy. You are a useful friend and relative," said Ngemwe as he joined him.

He was becoming tired of working from 5.30 a.m to around noon. He invited Mr. Gigali to his sitting place next to his house under a Mumogu tree. There was good shade, and the seats were well-prepared because that was where he sat when they were sharing the discussion with other colleagues; he also sat there during his leisure time. He, at times, also took meals from there. He called his elder child Muneri. "Muneri, Muneri," he said. "Yes, father," Muneri answered loudly. “Where are you?” asked Ngemwe. Muneri came carrying his younger sister Avambi. Before he could disclose what he had called Muneri for, Muneri explained, “I was preparing her lunch because the one my mother left was not enough because it was shared among others.” Ngemwe took Avambi and placed her on his lap; she was comfortable there.

Ngemwe told Muneri to enter his house and bring ripe bananas in a medium calabash under his bed, which he did. Then, he asked him to return and bring the remaining tea, to which he also obliged. Next, he told Muneri to call the other children, and when they came, he divided the bananas among them, each getting two, while the small children were each given one banana.

Mr. Ngemwe took one banana, peeled it, and gave it to Avambi to eat. He then handed her back to his brother. They were left with Mr. Gigali. He had instructed Muneri to go to the store and get eighteen eggs, boil them for the others and bring six to them. He gave him the key to the store. Mr. Gigali started taking ripe bananas while discussing with Mr. Ngemwe. They recalled the previous day's exercise at Avembe and how Ms. Urende frustrated them at the last minute.

Mr. Ngemwe told Mr. Gigali how he was optimistic about the case because they were fully prepared with his elder advocates. Mr. Jambaro, the prominent elder advocate, was the most astonished by the development of the case. He had come together with his grandson, who carried his personal effects, especially his four-legged stool. Mr. Gigali told him to make sure he contacted the chief's elders regularly to know the date of the case because if that was not done, there would be delays when his cows were grazing in a foreign land without the herders.

"My grandmother Aguelo used to tell us that when the medicine is stored outside, it becomes poison. I believe in this statement because the longer you stay without bringing master Tubelo home, the more you complicate the matter and chances of winning him to your side."

Mr. Gigali told him there were many ways of speeding the case process if properly prepared. For example, the chief, Mr. Biridu, or the chief's trustee and the chair of the chief's court elders, Mr. Mwandame, could be used to speed up the case process.

"All the clans and villages are represented, even if you want the information to be communicated in folded dry banana leaves." Muneri walked in holding a calabash. He placed the calabash beside his father and said to his father, "I have boiled them, and they are here." His father looked at him and asked, "Have you served the other children?" "Yes, everybody is taking their share as we speak," responded Muneri. "That is exactly how I told you to treat the young ones during the day when we are away," said the father.

Muneri left to accompany the other children in removing the shell from the egg. He met other children taking the share of the eggs he had given out to them. The children were very happy with the father, who had directed Muneri to prepare them boiled eggs during that time of the day. Mr. Ngemwe and Mr. Gigali discussed the case issue as they continued to eat ripe bananas and boiled eggs. Mr. Gigali commented that they had eaten a lot in the daytime when they should be working, and Mr. Ngemwe responded that what they were discussing was a very important subject affecting his life and that of his relatives or immediate family. He added that the discussion they carried out gave him a lot of information on how to approach the issue before him.

Mr. Gigali emphasised a lot on pushing the case using the relevant authorities, and he would get the answer as soon as possible. Mr. Gigali told him when he would plan to go and meet the chief or Mr. Mwandame at either the office or other places, including his home. He asked him to plan well and inform him three days in advance to complete his daily duties and mostly take care of the livestock at home, especially the cows, because the wife alone could not manage them as well as her household duties.

They discussed for about one hour, and Mr. Gigali was escorted to the main gate and left for home. He opened his gate and then went where the calves were feeding. He took more hay and gave the calves that were free in the compound. The calves were healthy, and Mr. Gigali was assured that the wife milked her share and left the calves with enough share. Hours and days had gone, and the elders were preparing the cases that had been postponed the previous Wednesday. The chair of the court was waiting for them that following Wednesday. But, again, days had gone, and Wednesday had turned up.

Chapter Thirteen

In the chief's compound, at around 8.00a.m., people were streaming into the compound. Elders and advocates of various parties accompanied their relatives and their parties. Several cases were to be heard on that day. The secretary made sure all the parties had attended. He called all who had cases to be heard that day. There was only one case of land boundary. The two parties had to pay fresh hearing fees. The plaintiff was Mr. Elaku from the Mukare clan, the respondent was Mr. Emakalo from the Akame clan, and both parties had their elders and witnesses ready. Mr. Emakalu was said to have extended the boundary of the land by twenty steps from the original boundary of the land. The initial boundary had been fixed by elders when the land was subdivided in the Mugari area. Several people and residents testified that the boundary was extended, and the Amakia council of elders were there to know how the truth of the matter would be arrived at.

The secretary Mr. Okimbwi made sure the venue was well-arranged. Few of the chief's elders had arrived, and those who had arrived were entering the chief's office for a consultation and other logistics. All people and parties were asked to be seated before the elders, and the chair took their seats. The three chief's elders, who had not arrived, were seen entering the gate and the chief's office as it was the tradition of the chief's elders. Other chief's guards were seated outside the office next to the chief's office and were in charge of the people locked in the chief's cells for that night. The chief's court was fully packed with those coming to hear their cases and present their cases, parties from all sides, their elders, and advocates.

Some had come to register new cases; others were coming to pay registration fees and would pay listening fees later. First, the chief's court chairperson and his elders came out of the chief's office led by the secretary, Mr. Okimbwi, and then two other elders, the treasurer, Mr. Queme, and the chairperson of the court, Mr. Mwandame, came out last. He stopped at the cell and spoke to the guard. After that, they both entered the chief's office. The court chairman was seen giving him some money to share with his colleagues who were left outside when they entered the office.

The chairperson came out of the office with the guard, and he was seen talking to the other guard and left for the case venue, which was about sixty metres away. All the people were waiting for him to arrive at the case venue. He left where they were talking with the guard and went to the place of the case. All the people, who were there, clapped their hands when he appeared before he sat on his seat among the other elders and in front of the crowd. Mr. Shindalu, the vice chairperson, was seated next to the court's chair, Mr. Mwandame; there was also the treasurer Mr. Queme on the other side of the chair, and Mr. Okimbwi, the secretary of the court, and the other elders from every clan in the community.

The secretary, Mr. Okimbwi, asked the people to be quiet because the cases were about to start. He asked all those who wanted to register the case to do so without wasting time. The registration fee was five hundred Dibari. "Are there people who want to register new cases to be heard by the chief's elders?" asked Okimbwi. "Yes," thundered the crowd. The treasurer Mr. Queme was seated in a separate place with a handbag where money was to be put after registration. Many people had come to register cases. When the chairman saw the long line of people, who had come to register cases, he returned to his office with his deputy Mr. Shindalu and the secretary. Then, they left for the office as they discussed issues in low tones.

The chairman called the chief's guard and asked him to open the cell and allow the prisoners to bask in the sun. He opened the cells, and six people came out. He explained to the chairman that several relatives had come to redeem their people, and he could see them in the meeting. So the chairman asked him to call them over. Many people gathered around the chairman, his vice-chairman, and the secretary. They surrounded them, and the chairman asked them to go under the Mungari tree for further discussion. Within a short time, many goats and sheep were brought to redeem prisoners from the cells before going to the police station and the court. The owners of the property were also there as regulation demanded.

The first person, who was arrested by the chief's guard having stolen a he-goat, had come to be redeemed with the he-goat of the same size that the owner had agreed and was accompanied by the Amakia Council of Elders. So many goats and sheep were brought or taken out of the chief's compound. Two of the six in cells were left because their cases were different. These were Mr. Ademe from the Akame clan and Mr. Mulevi from the Amakia clan. They had both destroyed crops belonging to Mr. Nebaro of the Athane clan and were arrested by the chief's representatives and his assistants the previous night after a violent resistance. They were properly disciplined by the chief's representatives and their assistants.

Their relatives had also agreed to pay for the bags the owners of the crops requested. However, it was subject to confirmation by the chief's elders. Afterward, the 'Amakia council of elders' member should take them to the elders for confession and report to the chief on the confession with the victim. The chairperson said if the culprit's father had agreed with the owner of the crops destroyed, they should wait for other processes to take place, and they would be free.

The guards were directed to keep them outside the cells until they met the relieving condition, and the guard nodded their heads in agreement. "We are waiting for their relatives, Mr. Chairman," one of the guards responded. There were still many people seated waiting for cases to start. However, they were very sure that each case would be taken care of.

One of the chief's elders went to where the chairman and his colleague were. "Mr. chairman, the registration is through. All new cases are registered." The chairman asked Mr. Shindali and another elder to join other people in the case. Those, who were seen basking in the sun, were also allowed to join after they met conditions set by the chief and his committee of elders.

When the chief returned, he asked the secretary to brief him on the new cases registered to know what common cases were in the location. There were:

- Two cases of land dispute,
- Three cases each of separation and divorce,
- One case of adultery,
- Three cases of child ownership,
- Five cases of non-payment of bride price,
- Seven cases of breach of agreement,
- Four cases of violation of barter,
- Five cases of breaching the Amakia council constitution and
- Two cases of breaching the Amakia council laws by asking for more bride price than the laws demanded.

The chairman asked the secretary to read the parties in each case. The parties were read, and the chairman asked the elders to fix the date of each case and divide each day equally. Then, the vice chairman, Mr. Shindalu, asked one of the ladies to lead with a word of prayer. Mrs. Adime took up the challenge, all the people stood up, and those with caps on their heads removed them. She conducted the prayers, and some of the people concluded with the words 'Anime,' others 'Good God,' others 'kinii ruki,' others 'mwanitha' and others 'Giyeti' and many other Godly praises.

The vice chairman thanked the people for turning up in good numbers and observing time. He promised the people that all their problems would be solved well and without gender bias, social status, nepotism, partisanship, and other related factors. The crowd clapped at the vice chairman even before completing his speech. The vice chairman invited the chairman of the chief's court to address the people. The chairman greeted the people, and there were clapping and ululations from the crowd. He asked them to listen to him carefully. He greeted the crowd again, and the people were clapping with a lot of happiness. He told the crowd that he was there to solve their problem, which cropped between themselves and those who refused what had been agreed upon by the majority, and laws were made by the majority.

"Cases are in this court because the applicant feels that the law has been bent not to favour him or her, which is why these cases are here. Traditionally, every society or community has laws and regulations to give them guidance or the way. If there are no laws and regulations, there is no society or community. We cannot behave like other animals; we are superior to other animals, even biblically where God created us in his image. What does the image in this context mean? Sorry, I am not challenging other religions when I talk from the bible. Accidentally or incidentally, I happen to be a Christian. I am not proclaiming Christianity as the best religion, but I belong to that religion," said the chairman.

The chairman told the crowd that he had asked the secretary to read the registered cases because he wanted to know what crimes people committed in the location and whether they were committed by the locals or others who joined them there. He said he was happy because the crime of robbery with violence and other violent crimes were not among them.

"Stealing is also scaling down. So many people had lost their goats when their relatives stole other people's goats because, like Hamurabi in Babylon, we have made our laws here which cost the thief an extra goat if caught and established the truth of the matter," said the chief.

"In the last one month, those, who had lost their goats to thieves, had an extra of forty-six goats to make the relatives of the victim bear that pain in them for proper advice and control," added the chairman. The chairman cautioned the people to avoid cases, no matter how small. He noted that many cases had been registered, meaning something was amiss.

The chairman stopped his speech from continuing with cases and sat down. All the people were attentive to the chairman's speech and clapped in appreciation. Then, the secretary called Mr. Elaku, the complainant against Mr. Emakalu from the Mukaru clan and Akame, respectively, who had a boundary dispute in the Mungari area. Mr. Elaku was called upon to present his case before the court elders and advocates. Next, Mr. Emakulu went before the elders, advocates, and other members of the public who were present at the venue. He said that he had a land at Mungari called Mungari Farm. He had harvested thirty-five bags of maize and twenty bags of beans on that land. “My neighbours are Mr. Okimbwi to the left, Mr. Pendare to the right, Mr. Quamee on the upper side, and Mr. Emakalu on the lower side. My clan Mukare gave this land to me six years ago; I fixed the corners of the boundary with stones buried down together with the jawbones of a bull in all the corners of the plot.

After the maize harvest last season, when I visited my farm, I met Mr. Emakalu, who had crossed the boundary and infringed on my land. I called my other neighbours to witness the extension of the boundary. I called Mr. Okimbwi, Mr. Pandare, and Mr. Quime, and they all turned up. I had also called Mr. Randi, my clansman and a member of the Amakia council of elders who witnessed when the clan handed over the land to me. He also got his land that way, and four plots of land separate us. Mr. Emakalu came to be my neighbour from the land sale of my clansman Mr. Sendala who migrated to the Akame clan four years ago, and I have called him my witness."

"I have also called the other clansmen who are in that clan and know my land's boundary. Furthermore, my wife, Idhama, knows where she was working before Mr. Emakalu extended the boundary. To conclude, Mr. Chairman, I am ready to be subjected to any traditional measure which is in force to reclaim my portion of land taken by Mr. Emakalu in Mungari.”

“Where is Mr. Emakalu? Can you dispute those allegations directed to you by Mr. Elaku?” asked the chairman. Mr. Emakalu said he bought the land three years ago from Mr. Sendala, a clansman of Mukare. “I came from Abame clan and bought it with one red bull which could cost three big he goats, three she-goats and one sheep, black in colour. They were presented to Mr. Sendala by my stepfather, the late Mr. Tebule, and Mr. Unendu, my friend who is here with me today as a witness to this case," responded Emakalu.

He claimed that he had never altered the boundary of the land nor used anybody to alter the boundary. The Chairman asked Mr. Emakalu whether he had anything additional to tell the court, and he said he did not have anything, though he had witnesses. The Chairman said that the case had been presented before the elders, the judges from all the parties. He asked them to ask any question, touching on any party. Still, the chairman asked all the people to follow the instructions and not abuse the rules and regulations of the court in force. He also asked the applicant and the respondent to answer the questions.

One person with long hair raised his hand and was allowed to speak. He asked Mr. Emakalu, "Mr. Emakalu, how old are you?" He was dragged out by the chief's guard before the chief objected to the question because the question was irrelevant. It was later known that he was a madman from the Akame clan who had followed the elders up to the chief's compound, attracted by the crowd he saw. He was dragged and taken outside the gate of the chief's court and was whipped for interrupting the court until people in the compound heard him yelling in pain. He ran fast towards where he had come to avoid the chief's security whips.

The chief's guard and security people went around the crowd to check whether other people of unsound minds were likely to interrupt the development of the court process. While inspecting and checking, two youths were caught by the collar of their shirts and dragged to the gate, then told to run without turning back. One of them was shabbily dressed and had shaggy hair, and the other was wearing two different shoes.

Mr. Verelo, an elder from Amugare, asked Mr. Emakalu whether he would admit to changing the boundary in dispute if the person, who sold to him the land, told the court that he extended the boundary to Elaku's land. "I did not extend the boundary," said Mr. Emekalu.

"Let us not waste time," said the chief. "Be direct and answer the way the question is put to you," said the chairman. "Mr. Verilo, can you repeat the question to Emakalu," asked the chairman. Mr. Verilo repeated the question to Mr. Emakalo, but he said there was a plan to take his portion of the land. The chairman again said that the question should be answered the way it was asked, and there should be no accusations, counter-accusations, or trade of blame games.

Mr. Wakambo wanted to know how long he had stayed with the boundary at the present position. Mr. Emakalo said that ever since he bought that land from Mr. Fendala. The chairman asked

Mr. Emakalu not to complicate himself in the case. The chairman said when a person wants to kill a snake; he hits the head and not any other body part.

The clansmen from the Elaku clan testified before the chief's court and said all the land given to the clansmen was measured with the steps of the people who are alive to date, and each land was eighty steps by one hundred and twenty steps.

Mr. Amande said that if any land was bigger than the others, it was that of the spokesman; it should be taken as a lie. He added that Mr. Sendala was not one of the spokesmen in the tribe and therefore did not benefit a step in addition from other members. Finally, he said he was ready to be subjected to any condition for what he had told the court. One of the elders nodded in appreciation of that last statement before the court.

He concluded by saying his statement was true and not intended to subject any party to loss but the truth of the matter the way he knew it from the ground. He then sat down.

The other elder, who was with Mr. Amande, made a different conclusion to say he should be subjected to any condition. He said so because Sendala was not a member of the council of elders and therefore could not commit himself to the law he did not know unless he was a member of the Amakia council of elders.

"The river is taking its course," said the chairman. Then, the chairman called Mr. Amande, the friend of Mr. Emekalu, and asked him whether he could identify the boundary they were shown when they were buying land, to which he responded he could not remember well. Next, another elder, Mr. Chabele, asked him whether he was a member of the Amakia council of elders. But he nodded his head because he was under interdiction for fighting his wife before her children in broad daylight.

People, who were there from his clan, doubted Chabele's statement but had not known that he was interdicted the previous week at a clan meeting. When Mr. Sandala was summoned by the chairman to testify in the case as the seller of that land to Mr. Emekalu, he said that he was the seller of that land to Emakalu. He also said that when the boundary was altered, he was called by Mr. Emakalu to witness the change. He also confirmed that the boundary had been extended towards his neighbour's land about five steps, which was a big portion of land the way we measured when we were getting portions of land from the clan.

He added that they had fixed the boundary with Emakalu, and they fixed the boundary with stones and the skulls of bulls. He said that he was ready to be subjected to any condition by the elders if need be in support of what he had said before the court and the elders.

"Mr. Chairman, I have concluded my statement before the court, and I stand by my statement firmly as the seller of that land," Emakalu stated.

All the elders looked at one another as if Sendala had concluded the case and had the final word to the case.

Mr. Emakalu wanted to say something, but the chairman told him that he had said enough when he was called to defend himself, and now it was a chance for their witnesses to testify. Both parties had closed their case. "They could only speak when asked anything by other parties in the case," added the Chairman.

Mr. Akelo requested the chairman to allow the wife, Mrs. Emakalo and Mrs. Ekalu to testify. Still, the chairman objected since their husband had already testified in the case before the elders, where women cannot be subjected to any condition based on the matter in question. "Well understood, Mr. Chairman," said Mr. Akelo. The chairman announced that if there was nothing to add to that case and the relevant parties were satisfied with what had been addressed before the chief's court, he would proceed to the next stage.

The chairman appointed three elders to go and view and confirm the boundary and bring the report five days later. And he said they should be accompanied by Mr. Emekalu, Mr. Okemburi, Mr. Pendame, Mr. Quime, and the chief's elders, Mr. Heburi from the Emulu clan, Mr. Liburi from the Ankire clan, and Mr. Mukubwa from Amugane clan. The chairman said while at the scene of the dispute, Mr. Liburi from the Ankire clan would be the chair.

The chairman added that they would also be accompanied by four security men from the chief's office with the power to arrest the person who would dispute the chairman's order, bring him into the chief's cell, and lock him up.

He also ordered the two parties to pay each three thousand Dibari viewing fee. "And nobody is allowed to carry anything in his hands, except the Amakia council of elders who should carry their official staff," said the chairman.

The chairman consulted Mr. Shindalu, and Mr. Shindalu asked Mr. Mwendame to lead with a closing prayer. All people stood up, and those, who had hats on, removed them except one old man dressed like a woman and had a Muslim cap. Mr. Mwendabe was an Amakia member, and he said the prayers in their tradition, and the members responded, "The Great one for us all, including our families, livestock, bless us all." This was the response from the Amakia council of elders to their prayer.

All the members of the Amakia council and other people, including the chief's elders, dispersed and left through the gate to their respective destinations at around 4.30p.m. Before the closing prayers were said, the chairman had announced that all the chief's court elders, security, youths and guards, and parents, who were coming to redeem their relative in the chief's cell, should wait for the chief who was on the way coming. There were people left behind who were affected by the announcement. The chairman and his elders were busy discussing the fate of those in the cells and their redemption procedure. There were about ten goats in the compound to pay the fee before the prisoners were set free. Before all the prisoners were freed, the chief arrived with two representatives and one security man armed with a plastic whip and a whistle hanging around his neck. All continuing activities stopped immediately when the chief entered the compound. He greeted the people in the compound by raising his official staff, and the people responded, "Omlembachee." He went straight to the office and was followed by the chief's court chairman and Mr. Shindalu but left the office shortly.

The chief stayed with the chairman of the elders for quite some time before he called other chief's court elders into the office. He had a small briefing session with them and sent Mr. Shindadu to call the chief's security men and the guards. They stayed in the office for official briefs and other unknown agendas from the chief. Finally, they all went out, and all the people in the compound were told to assemble under the tree, which was about twenty steps behind the chief's office. The chief greeted his subject a second time and congratulated his court elders on transparently conducting the local court because justice should prevail for all of them.

The chief asked the parents and the relatives to educate their people since they were to lose their livestock in the form of fines. "I have been briefed by my elders that already fifty goats are lost through stealing other people's goats as fines. Therefore, I am of the opinion that the elders should continue hearing the cases of how they are doing to discipline the culprit, offenders, and others bent on making other people suffer because they want to fulfill their wishes and hopes."

"If you happen to experience that, my elders are on the wrong track. Please may I know that secretly and I won't betray you," addressed the chief. "But up to now, we are clean," said the chief. And the chief added if there was anybody with a burning issue, he or she was at liberty to comment. The chief sat down and waited for comments, but there were none, and he asked the people to disperse. He was left behind with the court chairman, the deputy chairman, the secretary, and the treasurer. The security man and the guard were hanging around the chief's compound but not near the place where they were seated with the elders.

The chief asked for money from the treasurer, called the security men and guards, and gave each of them one hundred Dibari, and they left smiling. "We can now meet our families as happy husbands," said one of the guards.

After a short discussion, the chief and his leaders dispersed, and everybody went through the gate except for two young men who were left to guard the prisoners locked in the chief's cell. Two security men accompanied the chief to his home and then left to their homes. When the criminals and offenders went to meet the Amakia council of elders for confession, they paid a goat each before they could make morality confession before the Amakia council elders trusted from their respective families to the supreme council of elders.

One of the council's chief elders, Mr. Lembitu from the Athane clan, told the offenders, "You should not run away from justice because justice is not dead. You should face justice like men." He told them there was no society or community without its laws and justice, which is why there were the prisons, government courts, police, and even the chief's court.

"But since you are non-members of our council, you may not know your parents, and your relatives are not qualified to know for you." Mr. Muloro, from the Kigure clan, explained to the young men and referred to the council from the chief's court that anybody clever should be learned from other people or institutions like this one. "If one does not learn, that person cannot know what it is to be learned, and learning is continuous. Therefore, if one is learned in white man's education, then he is not learned in our school and therefore he is not qualified from our education and our school," Muloro added.

They were asked for their trustee Amakia elder from their respective clans and presented them. One of the offenders, Mr. Coanille's trustee Amakia elder, told the council, "The youth have always taken issues lightly in life, but they have known the other side of the coin. You cannot escape the police and the government court, where you meet a judge, like us, and judge you innocent or guilty. If these elders do not clear you, you face the music. These elders are your seniors in this particular case," said Mr. Fasse. "That is my message to you youths," he added.

There were six of them before the elders' court and five goats; one of them, Mr. Perali, had not brought his goat. He told the elders that his elder brother Mr. Hedari was bringing the he-goat or a sheep. The elders had to wait because the confession was taking place simultaneously, and their clearance was done. Three of the five goats were slaughtered, and a fire was lit, ready for the elders to enter the sacred groove to declare their clearance after confession. Elders were smeared with red ochre as a sign of officialdom.

Before the three goats were skinned, two elders and his brother Hedari, who was escorting the goat from behind, brought the goat for Mr. Perali. They confessed that the goat was the fee for Mr. Gerali's clearance, and it was tied together with the other two goats. The elders made them confess and entered the sacred groove to clear them from crimes. They were smeared with goat's fat on their forehead and the hands which handle property, and the mouth which eats as they repeated statements from the Amakia council of elders and cursed if they repeated the same crimes again.

They were also directed to curse themselves if they repeated the crime. Each cursed himself with his own mouth. Finally, the clearance was through, they were cleansed, five men from security officers were innocent, and five were among the community members. The final stage left was communicated to the chairman of the chief's court or the chief himself that the cleansing exercise was carried out after the confession.

This exercise took place at the Chilumi Amakia council of elders' sacred groove, where elders sat on the ground. Then, they were cleared, and one of the elders, Mr. Komolito, told them to report to the chairman of the chief's court elders on Wednesday before they started a case at Alembe chief's camp.

They were listening carefully, and they wanted to leave quickly. They were told to wait for the roasted meat. According to the number of elders present, one elder cut the meat into pieces. They were asked to sit separately from the elders, where they should be served pieces of roasted meat. One of them, Mr. Mwebuma, was handed the meat on a green banana leaf and asked to divide it among his colleagues, and the elder left to where others were seated waiting for their share.

The meat was divided among them by Mr. Mwebuma, and each of the six colleagues took his piece from the banana leaf. The meat was well-roasted, and a person could not finish two pieces. However, even one piece made a person satisfied.

The pieces comprised parts of the ribs, hips, and other parts of the body. They took the meat and were satisfied. They were not able to get all the meat from the piece that had big bones because they had no knife to enable them to extract the meat from the bones. However, the pieces of meat they were given were plenty for them to eat.

"These elders are generous; they have fed us with meat to our satisfaction," said one of the colleagues, Mr. Beridu. Moreover, the elders had eaten the meat of three goats and spared the other three to feed on another day. "There would be plenty of meat before them because about eighteen people had not been referred to them for confession and cleansing by the chief's court," added another colleague, Mr. Mwendeu.

One of them, Mr. Mwebuna, told the other that the elders ate meat every week in plenty because the chief's elders sat two times a week. Many people were referred to the Amaki, a council of elders, on Wednesdays and Fridays for confession and cleansing where there was a curse contrary to the tradition and culture of the people. There are cases where non–members conduct ceremonies contrary to the 'Amakia council of elders' regulations. They are forced to intervene and conduct the cleansing ceremony with a sheep or he-goat, as demands the issue in question.

They left the elders at the sacred grove and left for their homes. They went discussing how they would do all the way. They passed people on the sidewalk as they travelled. They discussed how they would meet on Wednesday morning to see the chairman of the court elders receive the final clearance together with the trustee elders.

They arranged to meet at Mambari swamp ground with their trustee elders to be presented at Avembe chief's camp for clearance from the chief's office. Mr. Abare, one of the Amakia council of elders, had been directed by the council to take them on Wednesday for final clearance at the chief's camp. So the young people had agreed to meet at the swamp ground to go with Mr. Abare.

Both Mr. Garrile and Mr. Adesu hailed from the Amalu clan, Mr. Porile from the Athane clan, Mr. Mwebure from the Antuambare clan, Mr. Ramisha from the Akame clan, and Mr. Remba from the Ankire clan. They were all happy to be cleared by the elders' council and knew their problems were solved. Mr. Adesu told the others that he would not repeat such a thing again, and he was likely to be initiated into the Amakia council of elders to be more transparent about crimes and other minor offenses.

Chapter Fourteen

On the following Wednesday morning, the six of them woke up very early in the morning and left for Avembe chief's camp. Some of them had woken up as early as 5:00a.m that morning. They travelled to Avembe chief's camp, each from his own home, and arrived at Mambari swamp ground. Five of them met at around 7:00a.m. Unfortunately, Mr. Remba from the Ankire clan had not arrived, and the presenting elder had also not arrived at the ground.

As they were talking, they saw Mr. Rembo coming from the direction of his home. He came and greeted them in the local language, "Adumbe," greeted Mr. Rembo. "Wendumba o Rembo," responded his five colleagues. They sat on the stones waiting for Mr. Abare. After ten minutes, they saw Mr. Abare approaching from the eastern direction holding an elder's staff in his right hand and walking leisurely in short steps.

They were discussing how happy they would be when they received the final clearance. Finally, Mr. Abare reached where they were seated and greeted them, "Adumba oluma." "Adumba zika," responded the young men.

"You mean you are as serious as you promised?" Abure asked.

"Yes, we want to move from insecurity areas in crimes," responded Mr. Adesu. Mr. Abure told them that it would be known from their activities sooner or later. He told them they had been treading on dangerous ground that would tarnish them locally and spoil their future. "You have lost a lot of wealth from your families, which cannot be recovered soon," said Mr. Abure. "Unless you are a changed person, you will be no more," added Mr. Abure.

They all started walking to Avembe chief's camp. They all discussed as they walked to their destination. The young people felt guilty about stealing the goat and losing the other two as fines and clearance fees by the elders. They felt that they had subjected their family to great loss economically. Mr. Abure told them they would be put under the surveillance of the chief's security team in their respective areas after clearance from his office.

“The chief has many eyes and ears to identify you and others who are suspected of various crimes in the location and even beyond,” said Mr. Abure to the young people. He told them that the chairman of the court or the chief, whoever they met, might interview each of them for some time to gauge their repentance, future activities, and innocence.

Mr. Abure continued to tell them that their social records had been affected even before public eyes and would be questioned by the public unless there was a total change which was beyond doubt. "My grandfather used to tell us that the child, who has not fought his father physically, is better than the one who has fought him physically and repented with a he-goat."

“Here is a son who has never repented for doing nothing, and here is another son who has repented for doing something, who has a better degree of morality?” asked Mr. Abure. But unfortunately, six of the young men were not in a position to answer the question put to them.

They passed river Tithe as they walked that morning and passed the Mboroko ranges. Mr. Abure asked them if they were serious about changing their behaviour and attitude as they promised in their clearance exercise. They kept quiet and said they were ready to change for their good. He continued to tell them that he wondered whether it was an accident or incident that lured them into that trap. Mr. Abure told them that clearance was as important as changing the social attitude and behaviour before the community and security one was living in.

After walking for about four kilometres, they were joined by other people. Some were elders who had Amakia elders' staffs. All, who had the staff, greeted Abure with Amakia elders' language and after greeting his elder colleague, finally, greeted the young people with the ordinary language. They learned that the council group was popular and respected in the clans and community at large. There were many people on the way because it was approaching 8:00a.m.

There were groups of men walking with either one, two, or three elders with a staff signifying that that group had a case, and they were accompanied by the elders who would present themselves as elders' advocates before the court. There were more people on the way as time ticked. "We are about to arrive; let us stop somewhere before we reach the gate of the chief's compound," said Mr. Abure. So they went a few steps and stopped.

He advised them to keep behind him when they arrived at the chief's compound until they entered the chief's office. "I will know when we should enter the office or not," said Mr. Abure. "And don't discuss anything with anybody until we complete this process," added Mr. Abure. When they reached the chief's camp, many people were in the compound, and the office was open, but people were neither entering the office nor were any people near the office door. So they entered the gate and went towards the chief's office behind the elder leading them.

Mr. Abure asked them to wait until he called them into the office. He went to the office and knocked, although it was open. He entered, leaning on his staff that the young man thought he would leave outside the office. Many people looked at the young men who were standing in one place. Many suspected they were going for final clearance because they were locked in the cell the previous week.

After staying inside for ten minutes, Mr. Abure stood at the door, and then beckoned them to come. He held Mr. Adisu by the left shoulder, forced him into the office, and beckoned others to go where they were standing. He was interviewed by the court chairman, who was there with the treasurer for about ten minutes, and went outside the office. After that, Mr. Rumela entered and came out after fifteen minutes. They were all interviewed and given the final clearance.

After the interview with the elder who brought them to the office, the court chairman called all of them and told them, "You have been cleared by this office from now but placed under probation for three years. So we have the eyes to see where you are and what you are doing for that period, and then we can decide whether the office will confirm your innocence and free you or not," said the chairman with authority.

"Mr. Abure, you are in the council where all the clans are represented. Report their behaviour and attitude to this office every four weeks with effect from now," said the chairman to Mr. Abure. Mr. Abure assured the chairman that he would follow them day and night through his Amakia elders' agents. "Thank you, Mr. Chairman," Abure bent his head and left the office with the six young men.

As they were about to reach the compound, one of the court elders caught up with them before they reached the gate and told them they had not paid the cell's guard fee of fifty Dibari each for the two days they had stayed there. They contributed and paid six hundred Dibari, which was handed over to the treasurer. When they reached and passed the gate, they ran as fast as if being chased away from the chief's compound. People, who went with them, had to take the sidewalk.

Mr. Abure told them not to run and wait for him, but they could not wait for him. They went to wait for him far away from the camp to avoid the possibility of being called back. "These are things I did not know, be careful," directed Mr. Abure to the young men. Abure told them because they were parting within a short distance from where they were; they wished each other goodbye. "Go and share with your people and relatives the experience you have undergone to know this world better. Greet your parents," added Mr. Abure and left alone on the road that led to the eastern side. He left them standing at the junction where he parted with them.

The young men talked a bit about their experience in the chief's cell and what they had paid as fees to the elders, penalties, and especially a goat; they recounted and saw they had subjected their family and relatives to a great loss. They also agreed that they should leave that job and join a good job without shame, stress, and the physical problem they had experienced, including shame and loss of material property.

They also parted ways; Mr. Gerille and Mr. Adesu followed the route to the north; Mr. Gerille followed the north-western route,

Mr. Mwebuma followed the southern route, Mr. Pamba left for the southwest, and Mr. Lemba followed the north-western route.

They all left silently and alone except for Gerille, who was accompanied by his colleague Mr. Adesu. Some of them were waving hands in the air when they tried to calculate the cost of the case. Two people were left in the chief's cells for lack of the required fees and penalty, and they were taken to the police station, threw them to the court of law, and jailed for two and a half years each. Most people applauded the chief because the considerable magnitude of crimes was reducing in number in the location, and most subjects were law-abiding citizens.

Chapter Fifteen

When Master Alevi returned home, he met the house opened and suspected that his brother was not there. His mother brought Master Alevi food on a plate and another for his brother, Pumela. "Keep the food safe for Pumela," his mother told him. He took both plates, put Pumela's next to his bed, and started taking his meal. Master Pumela came with green leaves for the goats and put them in their enclosure for them to feed on. He entered the house and greeted Master Alevi. He saw that he was in a gloomy mood and did not want to talk to him or ask him any questions. He suspected that he was berated by his father because the father did not side with anybody who did not follow his instructions.

He showed him his food next to where he slept. The bed had been empty for two days since the chief's security men arrested him as he was coming home. His father did not know until the next day when the owner of the goat he had stolen was traced in his maize plantation, where he was weeding in the afternoon session. He was angry because of how his mother scolded him and his father, who had planned his expulsion from the family using the chief and his council of elders who would withdraw his clan membership and expel him to another clan for his crime attitude and behaviour.

His mother, Maridama, who was brewing millet gruel in the house, commented, "Alevi, I don't want you to walk in this company because it is said if you walk in the company of a thief, you also become a thief, look at my goats, where did you take them?" When Pumela heard that, he became gloomier; he looked down as he took food and porridge. His parents, especially his father, subjected him to guilt conscious at the comments he made.

The other thing is that he had lost property that was family property, including the three goats he had paid for, and therefore what the parents were saying was the truth. Payment of the two goats had subjected the family to loss of its wealth. The other thing is the animals in the tradition of Amakia people constituted part of the bride's wealth.

There were many reasons for the parents to be angry with Pumela, their son, which he should consider. But instead, he started taking his share of the meal, nursing his gloominess.

His brother Alevi finished taking his lunch, took the panga, and left for his mother's beans and banana garden, where he worked before coming for lunch. "Have you cleared the weeds at the left corner of the garden?" Maridama asked her son Alevi. “I cleared that in the early hour of the day,” replied Master Alevi. Master Alevi proceeded to the garden and left Pumela behind in the house, taking his lunch and his father mending the fence.

When the father realised he had finished eating, he went near their house and told Pumela, “Take the panga and follow your brother to the garden." He heard what his father told him and followed his brother to the beans garden. He met his brother working in the portion planted with beans, and his brother Alevi showed him where to start working with a panga.

He bent and started working, removing the weeds from the beans plants. Nobody spoke in the family, including his young brother and his sister, because his father was a serious man and could fight him for losing the goats to the chief and Amakia council of elders when he was not initiated into their membership. So they worked in the garden until they completed the portion planted with beans that the mother wanted to be cleared.

They turned to the portion planted with black beans, which was bigger than the one planted with beans, and completed it before they left for home at 6.30 p.m. When Master Alevi arrived home, his mother asked how far he had worked. "I had completed the portion planted with beans which I was assisted by Master Pumela when he came and turned to the portion planted with black beans, and we have also completed in the late hours of the day."

“Where is he now?” asked the mother.

“I have left him on the way coming,” he replied.

“Meet him and tell him to come and not to respond anything negative to your father; let him do what he asks him to do until the history of his lost goats subsides. Let him not leave the compound unless he is sent or leaves to work in the family garden,” said the mother. “Have you clearly understood me?” repeated the mother.

"Yes, mother," responded Alevi.

He left the compound quickly, met his brother on the way, and stopped him to convey his mother's message. However, he did not ask him whether he heard the news right because he feared confronting him because of that bitterness and the unfriendly language from his parents and especially his father, who sacrificed his property for his release from the chief's cells and clearance from the elders.

His brother Alevi went back ahead of him and met his father seated on his three-legged stool, and he asked him, "Is your brother lost again?"

“No, he is coming slowly from the garden where we were working with him,” responded Alevi.

The father sat looking in the direction of the gate. He heard the sound of the gate and saw him closing it and coming towards their house. He kept the panga outside and entered the house. His father could not hear any word from any of them. Master Alevi came out and asked the mother for water to wash. "To wash the whole body or just your hands?" asked his mother.

All this time, the father was sitting near their mother's house, which was the sleeping house and kitchen. This was also where the chicken spent their night. Master Alevi told the mother that he needed water to wash his hands and feet. She brought water in a medium gourd and a metal utensil and kept them next to his son’s house. The mother called Master Alevi from the house and told him that she had brought the water. Master Alevi poured water into the metal container and started washing his hands and feet while he was still standing. “Take a seat and wash well,” directed his father.

His father sent his young sister with a circular woodcut on both sides, which his father had cut out with an axe to serve as a seat in the living room. It was also used as a seat outside. The young children liked sitting on it while waiting for supper and warming themselves at the side of the hearth in the mornings. The young sister returned to the mother's house, preparing the evening meal. The mother sent her with roasted bananas to take to the father, who was seated outside. When she returned to the house, she sent her with others to take to Alevi and his brother Mumela.

The sister had not seen Mumela for two days, and when she saw him, she asked, “Mumela, when did you come, and where were you? I have not seen you for two days." He took it as an insult because she asked in the language of his father, and he did not want his father to be reminded of the ugly incident and especially the loss of his goats that were lost by him. So he did not answer, and she repeated, "Mumela, where were you for two days? Alevi was sleeping alone in the house.”

The mother heard the question got unanswered and called her quickly to avoid subjecting him to more stress and bitterness from the father who was hearing what was transpiring.

Alevi did not want her to reflect on the past with Mumela and his father, who were enemies because of Mumela’s character, which his father called a crooked character. So when the younger sister returned to her mother in the main house, the mother told Chadilo not to ask Mumela any question until three days were over and she would tell her where he was. "When you go there, especially while taking food to them, don't ask them questions; they are circumcised boys. Children, do not ask circumcised boys questions. Is that clear?" emphasised the mother.

"Why, mother, why don't they answer questions?" asked Chadilo. After eating the roasted bananas, the mother promised to answer that question. She also gave Chadilo two roasted bananas and directed her where to sit as she took the roasted bananas. Then, the mother started lecturing Chadilo about the fire and cooking pot to divert her attention from her brothers, especially his whereabouts, and why children do not ask questions to circumcised boys.

The mother prepared food and served it to the family members equally. The mother sent Chadilo first to take food to the father, who had left for his house on the left side of their house, where they slept with the mother, and then to her brothers, whose house was a bit far from other houses.

The mother escorted her and stood at a distance because she feared the darkness. She took the food twice because she could not carry the two plates at once. Finally, the mother asked if she would do what she had told her not to do. She did exactly what she was told by her mother. When she took the food, she only looked at Mumela with fixed eyes, and Mumela suspected the reason for doing it.

“Are they all there?” asked the mother to Chadilo. “Yes, and Mumela is seated on his bed quietly,” responded Chadilo. “And who is Alevi talking to?" asked the mother. "He asked me if the food has enough salt, and I told him I saw you add some salt while preparing," said Chadilo. The mother laughed lightly and asked her to take her share of her food. Before Maidala took her share, she went out and checked whether the cows were properly locked in their enclosures and whether they were all there.

She came back with her daughter Chidalo who did not want to be left in the house alone for fear of darkness. She walked behind her mother, holding her dress as they walked to and from the cows' enclosures. She kept close to the mother as she lit a fire in the house when they returned from the cows' enclosures. The mother told her the stories of the source of darkness, the owner of the house, the children, and the night.

When morning dawned, Mr. Muvendwa called his wife Maridhama to his house, and after a short discussion, they concluded that Mumela should be married soon after Alevi’s wife reported home. He told his wife that he was irresponsible because he had no responsibilities. "Let him marry his wife to share the responsibilities of the home and head his family, and if he repeats what he did previously, I can expel him with his wife," the father told the mother. "I want him to split the trees behind your house for his house, and I will provide him with all that is needed for the house. I want him to have a separate compound and his own gate; I do not want him to use my gate after he has built his home and married his wife. He has ashamed me before my age grade, and the family is no more," added Mr. Muvendwa.

He added that after marrying, he might pay for more livestock and get him initiated into the Amakia council of elders group to clear the family from his shame. The wife did not comment to attract his anger but listened to him carefully and attentively to avoid chaos in the family. Maridhama suggested that the husband marry him first and wait for him to have children before he was initiated to the Amakia council of elders. She told the husband that the family would be working for people who would be using their sweat.

“You have said, and you can observe and judge a situation,” responded the husband. “Let us now hurriedly marry Alevi and bring his wife home. I will build his house within two weeks and should be within this compound and would be using that gate," said the husband angrily as he pointed at the gate. Finally, they agreed with his wife about what they would do to both of their sons. Then, the wife left for her house to prepare for the day.

Master Mumela was listening to that morning attentively to the discussion between the father and the mother, but since his father's house was at a distance, he had not heard everything. When the mother left his father's house, they suspected all was not well because of her facial appearance, but she could not reveal the secret. She always told them to listen attentively to the father and implement his words, but this was not the case with Mumela.

They could not talk to each other because they did not know what in store for them was; his father could order them to build their houses in their own compound and leave his compound within the same plot. However, they did not know whether that could happen to the unmarried man. Master Alevi was afraid and angry with his brother, who was the source of the problem which might affect him. He knew he had not committed any crime whatsoever but did not know his fate when judgement would be passed by the head of the family. He had been angry and gloomy for the last two days since the arrest of Master Mumela.

The mother came from his father's house with a face that reflected an unhappy mood which made her sons suspect all was not well in that compound. However, they knew their father had communicated to the mother in an unpleasing language, which she could not approve of, and she allowed free judgement. Master

Alevi took tea and roasted bananas as their usual breakfast with his brother, and they both left to work on her garden as they had promised their mother the previous night.

Their neighbour, Mr. Dambori, came to meet Mr. Muvendwa that morning to hear the fate of his son, who was arrested by the chief's security men for allegedly stealing a goat belonging to Mr. Gambodi from the Amugane clan, the neighbouring clan, when they were grazing in the wilderness. When he inquired from him, before he answered what Mr. Dambori was asking, he responded, "This is a shame especially and mostly from a family like this one, when I am an elder of Amakia council. That is why I paid for all the goats and other material requirements without questioning; what do I question if I do not know our people's traditional and cultural laws? Soon after my marriage, I became a group member; my mother paid several gourds of gruel and cooked food during my seclusion days. So I am planning how to do away with this shame," said Mr. Muvendwa.

They discussed a bit, and when Mr. Dambori noticed that his friend was not in his usual mood, he left him in his compound. The chief had a locational meeting that Saturday, and the meeting was well-announced by his representatives in various areas of the location. All leaders in the location were asked to attend the meeting. The meeting was to take a few hours if people reported early. The chief had announced that he would report at Gambole primary school ground at exactly 10.30 a.m to address the meeting and allow people to go on with their businesses.

When the day broke, the chief arrived at about 9.30 a.m accompanied by assistant chiefs Mr. Amaro and Buchure from Libuni and Nemburi sub-locations, respectively. They were also accompanied by senior chief representatives, Mr. Chebiro, Mr. Dhambu, and Ebaki from Okila, Ramberi, and Quamata sub-locations. When they arrived, they met the Chairman of the chief's court elder,

Mr. Mwandame, the assistant chief of Chalana sub-location, where the meeting was to take place,

Mr. Mwambaro Keli was accompanied by his guard and his security Mr. Akemba, youth wing leader Mr. Mbetoro and women representative Mrs. Dambelo, and Amakia council of elder members from that area Mr. Akembo.

The venue was well-arranged by the assistant chief of that area, assisted by his people. They had carried chairs and tables in the classes and were well-arranged at the sitting place with the big chair, which was spread with red material for the chief, and the table was also spread with blue material. On the right hand of the chief's seat were three seats and on the left were three seats as well. Behind the chief's seat were many seats arranged in rows of five each. The assistant chief sat on the right side of the chief's seat, readily waiting for him to arrive. The chief's entourage was shown where to take their seats by the assistant chief Chalana sub-location. He greeted the chief with a salute and directed him to his seat. He was followed by several assistant chiefs; he also showed them where to sit in the front row where the chief was seated.

Mr. Mwandame, the chairman of the chief's court, was seated directly behind the chief, and next to him on the right was his assistant Mr. Shindalu, followed by the court's treasurer, Mr. Queme; and the secretary of the court, Mr. Okimbi. Next, on the left side of Mr. Mwandame was the chairman of the chief's security men, Mr. Hadharima; his assistant, Mr. Jodibe; the treasurer, Mr. Limboki and the secretary, Mr. Kombari. Then, on the other back row, there were the chairman of the guard, Mr. Manande; his assistant, Mr. Nimboko; treasurer, Mr. Odibe; and the secretary, Mr. Ponde.

'The Amakia council of elders' was also represented by the chief's elder and chairman Zeem Muloro from the Kigure clan, the assistant Mr. Qondele; treasurer, Mr. Shindambo; and the secretary, Mr. Timbonelo. The other leaders were women representatives, the chairperson, Mrs. Abande; vice chairperson, Mrs. Bonde; the treasurer; Miss Chede; and the secretary, Miss Dabiro. Sitting on the last row were the youth chairman, Mr. Edombe, vice chairperson, Miss Fadele; treasurer, Mr. Gakembo; and the secretary, Miss Habolo.

Before the chief and his entourage arrived, the assistant chief of that area, Mr. Mwambaro Keli, had already arranged his residents and how they would receive the chief and his entourage.

He had also directed them to attend the meeting in good number to pledge their loyalty to the chief and the government of the day. In addition, he had directed them to prepare their home early in the morning to get time to attend the chief's meeting. He had also asked them to set aside the day for that occasion and not mix it with other duties. "The chief's meetings are rare in the sub-location, or they may be none. So why don't you all come to buy your freedom from him? When you demonstrate that you are loyal to him, he will be looking at you with one eye when others are looked at with both eyes," the assistant chief told his residents.

There were many residents from the hosting sub-location and others from other sub-locations in the Maboro location. "Leaders were as many as the residents in that meeting," exaggerated Mr. Ndombo from the Ankire clan. The residents arrived at the meeting venue minute after minute. The chief and his assistants wore bright uniforms with a crown that reflected against the morning sun. The assistant chief, who hosted the meeting, went to where the chief was seated, made some consultations, and went back to arrange people who had come for the meeting. The chief also wore a spotted jungle jacket that made him smarter and more attractive to the public eyes than usual.

After a few minutes, the chief beckoned the hosting assistant chief. They were seen consulting quietly. The only people who could hear what they were saying were the leaders seated near them. The hosting assistant chief turned on the back and front and clapped his hands to attract people's attention. All the people looked in his direction. He looked at the sun that was shedding light from an angle of about forty-five degrees. He greeted the people and said the meeting was about to start because the chief of the location was there with his entourage and other leaders from the location.

"These are our leaders, but I wouldn't like to present the chief because that is the time of his agenda. Mine is not speaking now, but I welcome the location chief to address his subjects and what he has for us in this location. I will ask all seated to stand up to welcome the chief," the assistant chief said. All the people stood up.

All the people in the meeting clapped and ululated so loud that that could be heard from a long distance, making the hosting assistant chief smile. The chief walked a few steps from where he was standing and greeted the people. "Vulembi Omadu," greeted the chief. "Alembi Chamawe Zebu," responded the crowd in a thunderous sound that seemed to deafen some people's ears, including the chief. Nevertheless, the chief was happy with the turnout and the reception, including the arrangement of the place they were seated.

The residents were many, and they sat in the field. The chief was happy with the leaders because the members represented all the departments. There was the representation of the chief's court, the security personnel, and the guard of the cells, the Amakia council of elders, women representatives, and youth.

'The Amakia council of elders' was represented by old people. They were carrying the official staff and were not making noise, unlike other groups seated behind the chief. They talked and discussed in low tones. The chief started to address the meeting and said he was impressed by the turnout of the meeting with their reception when he arrived and started addressing them.

"Before I say why I have come here, may I introduce leaders who work with me and your people?" said the chief. He started with the hosting assistant chief, and there were claps everywhere. The assistant chiefs were followed by the chief's court elders, who made people clap, and the chief could not control them, and when they stopped clapping, there were murmurs here and there. Finally, the chief said, "I will keep quiet and sit until you stop murmuring." As he smiled immediately, the murmurs subsided.

The chief asked his court elders to stand up, and there was clapping again from the crowd. All the residents murmured and pointed to where Mr. Mwandame was seated.

"Thank you, my residents. If it was not for our good job together, you cannot express your happiness that way through your claps," said the chief.

The chief said, "Before you here is the chairman of my court elders, Mr. Mwandame." Before the chief pronounced his name, there was clapping and ululation, and even other leaders, including the assistant chiefs, fixed their eyes on Mr. Mwandame as if he were a stranger or had taken a transformation. Then, there was a lot of murmuring again, and the chief was interrupted by the noise. Some short people, who were seated, also stood up to see Mwandame prompting other people to also stand. Finally, some people asked the chief to repeat his name. "I said Mwandame," repeated the chief.

When the noise and murmurs subsided, the chief introduced Mr. Shindalu; the assistant of Mr. Mwandame; the treasurer, Mr. Queme; and the secretary, Mr. Okimbwi. The chief told them other members were not there. "Let us know their names," shouted people from different directions in the meeting. The chief rose and asked Mr. Mwandame to tell them the names of the other members. He announced the names of others, and there was clapping and ululations, and Mr. Mwandame and his team, as well as the chief, were happy and appreciated the good work of the chief's court.

The assistant chief stood and greeted the people, and he was welcomed with claps from all corners of the field. He welcomed the people and his colleagues in this location, mainly the chief, who decided to come and educate his people despite the tight programme in his office. The assistant chief introduced his staff and the other leaders he worked with. He introduced the chairman of security, Mr. Mande, and his team from sub-areas and the education team who checked on parents whose children did not attend school and followed school equipment stolen from schools. The education team also identified children who needed money to continue their education and follow healthy lifestyles, and the environment committee saw that all families had pit latrines.

"Those are the people I work with, Mr. Chief," concluded Mr. Mwambaro Keli.

The chief summoned his neighbour on the left, Mr. Amoru, from the Libuni sub-location. He thanked the chief for bringing him to the sub-location where the people were very good banana farmers; he also thanked people for giving them a very good reception. He sat down. The assistant chief Nemberi sub-location was the next to speak. He thanked the chief who had called the meeting at that venue for them to familiarise themselves with the location. The assistant chief, the host, the leaders of the location who had turned up in big numbers, and especially the Amakia council of elders who were elderly and made sure they attended the chief's meeting despite their age. The people also turned up in good numbers to tell the leaders in the security system that they supported them morally.

"May I lastly thank the residents of this sub-location and their leaders, my colleagues, for coming early and in good numbers to attend the chief's meeting? Our chief, I beg to stop with those many remarks, Sir." Next was the assistant chief Nemburi sub-location Mr. Mwelimo. Mr. Mwadime greeted all the people present and congratulated all the people for attending the meeting and arriving on time. He mostly thanked the good work done by the chief's court members and the Amakia council of elders. "*The Amakia council of elders* is making our work easier by following crimes and criminals within their border. May I thank everybody again for attending this meeting?" thanked Mwelimo.

It was the turn of assistant chief Mwetere sub-location, Mr. Korebo, who was also a neighbour to the host. He thanked everybody for attending the chief's meeting and especially the Amakia council of elders who were aged. He thanked them again for dealing with criminals and other evil-doers in their court. The assistant chief also thanked all the committees in the location and mostly the chief's court, who listened to cases they decided were acceptable to the residents and disciplined the wrongdoers together with the security committee who assisted in the administration of justice. The chief was also thanked for creating that department to curb crimes, assist the government in curbing crimes in the sub-locations, and create room for peace and development. Finally, he stopped there and wished success to the residents of the location.

Mr. Munoli, the assistant chief of the Jamali sub-location, thanked the chief and other people for attending the chief's meeting and thanked the chief for forming the committee and departments in his location, which did a lot to curb crimes and others in the location. The chief, he said, had played a great role in delivering justice and listening to the local disputes which emanated from the residents. He also praised other departments and committees, especially the security committee, which had reduced the crimes that the chief's court listened to and then referred to the Amakia council of elders for further action.

"Many cases of crimes have been solved here, and the listening and judgment have been acceptable by the local leaders and the people themselves. Likewise, the courts and elders are acceptable to the residents and community. May I pray for the same spirit to continue, and I thank all the leaders and the residents," said Mr. Munoli. Last but not least was the assistant chief Kande sub-location, Mr. Zembule. The assistant chief thanked everybody for coming to the meeting and thanked all committees in the location for good work done.

He especially congratulated the chief's court elders on listening to the cases and delivering judgment without bias against anybody and without fear or favour. When people heard this, they clapped for the assistant chief and shouted, "Mwandame, Mwandame." The security committee was also thanked for delivering peace in the location and arresting criminals locked in the chief's cells and forwarded to the police station, the chief's courts, and the Amakia elders' court. The assistant chief praised these local institutions for doing the right thing when people wanted peace and justice within their surroundings and environment.

"May I ask all the committee and the chief's court, in particular, to keep up?" the assistant chief concluded.

The chief invited the chairman of the court, Mr. Mwandame, and there was clapping and happiness among the residents in the meeting. When Mr. Mwandame rose from where he was seated to come in front to speak, people clapped and cheered him loudly, but that was expected. The leaders, especially the chief, and his assistant chiefs, knew the residents liked the administration of justice in the chief's court under the chairmanship of Mwandame. So Mr. Mwandame stood and greeted the residents while waving to them because he was not a person with a loud voice.

The crowd applauded him happily. He thanked the chief for calling them to the meeting with his executive. He told the court that they were appointed by the chief from every clan, representing the seven clans in the location. They represented Amalu, Athane, Antumbane, Akame, Ankire, Amarare, and Mukare clans. He thanked the chief and his elders for listening to the cases and trying their best to judge them using the highest degree of fairness and standard.

"Some cases are difficult to judge, but we manage and are all members of the Amakia council of elders. That is why we can judge cases because we apply the traditional custom and cultural law and constitution."

He told the crowd that other cases were referred to by the chief or assistant chief to the Amakia council of elders or to the court for listening and arbitration. He said, "Some cases are brought to us but with the approval and blessing of the chief. Other cases are brought to the court by individual members or a group of people like a family, village or a clan against another clan." He said the nature of cases included murder, robbery with violence, robbery without violence, stealing, witchcraft, marriage, divorce and separation, custody of children, and bride price. The other cases which they dealt with were small and medium.

Mr. Mwandame told the residents that cases are held on Wednesdays and Fridays all the weeks except December, when they take a recess for twenty days from 10th December. He asked people to avoid crimes, especially because many people had wasted time in court; others had wasted a lot of time in prison together with property in court and Amakia elders' court when judged guilty. "There are others who steal other people's property like livestock, and we have many cases of stealing goats, mostly when they are grazing in the field with children. Those, who have been identified, have paid for three goats, one for returning to the owner, another is fine, and the other one has been given to Amakia elders who conduct confession on you and clear you. And this has been agreed upon in a meeting by all of you; hence, some of you are victims of circumstances directly or indirectly."

"Some parents and relatives claim to have lost three goats but don't say where they lost the three goats. A person should say my son or relatives stole somebody's goat and were forced to pay for three goats. Suppose one cannot administer his family or talk to the relative who steals other people's property, and you are brought before us. In that case, we shall listen to your argument and judge your case by what is agreed by the residents and judge you accordingly."

"We have many people in court and others serving jail sentences today. Right now, as I sit here, there are people in chief's cells, police cells, courts, and others having been found guilty in the court of law and are serving a jail sentence. In addition, do not forget that others are awaiting their case from us, and others are waiting to be heard by the Amakia council of elders for many cases. May I present the council of elders who are here and can present their views to you? But I know they deal with cases, including criminal cases of various natures from the Amakia community and beyond. The chairman Zeem Muloro was here, and I heard him hint some issues, and maybe he will say more next time," said Mr. Mwandame.

“In our court today,” the chairman said, “there is reporting fee, registration fee, and adjournment fee. In addition, there is another fee, called claiming fee which is claimed to win property from the opposing party if you win your case. This is what is said. And when you come for the case after adjournment, one pays the registration fee because the elders cannot stay without their meals throughout the day serving you. They could be assisting with duties at their homes."

"When you are coming to the court, you must be prepared with fees, your elders' advocates, and witnesses to avoid inconvenience. You should also be prepared because the case may demand being referred to the Amakia council of elders, where we have no facilities in our court. One should be prepared to attend their court case like witchcraft, if the accused denies before our court, we refer you to them who will know what to do immediately after hearing the allegation or nature of the offense," said the chairman.

The chairman told the residents that the council of elders from the Amakia team becomes simpler if the accused party is their member. However, these are rare and discouraged cases of elders. Mostly men are the most qualified to be listened to in their court. He said there were many issues he would have liked to brief the people and begged to sit.

People were happy to hear from him and clapped after he concluded his speech. Then, the chairman of security, Mr. Mwandame, was asked to say something. He greeted everybody in the meeting and introduced himself a second time. He said their job was the most difficult because they dealt with difficult people, complex cases, and situations. In addition, he said they dealt with armed criminals who could kill or cause injury while making arrests.

"We track and follow the criminals as long as they are here in our location, and if you cross our boundary, you pray to God until you come back in Amakia. Then, we shall leave to our agents messages of your reporting to Amakia either day or night, and if we suspect that those who have made contact with you or hiding a criminal are not ready to report the crime. Then, we report to the chief, and the chief refers you to the Amakia council of elders where you deny before them, and they would judge and administer the case accordingly," said the chairman.

"There are cases where an alleged criminal becomes violent and resists arrest; we must arrest, we follow you, chase you, and it has been agreed that a criminal must be arrested by all, including you, to assist us when we are making an arrest because it is for your good and security that we are doing it," said the chairman of security.

The chairman showed scars he sustained while making the arrest and some of his security men had the same scars. "In every village," the chairman said, "there were three security men." He also said if they knew the criminal might cause trouble to arrest or had dangerous arms, they involved the administration policemen or regular policemen and ensured the alleged criminal was arrested. A case like that one was directly taken to the police station and then to the court of law in Alandi or Mukurui for further administrative action from the government magistrate.

The chairman told the people that he had confidence in his team because there was no case that had not been dealt with, and they make arrests at night and in any kind of weather if the occasion demands.

"We are not employed by the government, we have no salaries, but we assist in eliminating criminals here for peace and development of the location." The chief nodded in acceptance. People clapped for the chairman and murmured to appreciate the good work. Most people said that they slept peacefully and without suspicion of theft or any other dangerous form of crime in their villages and families.

He also congratulated and thanked the residents for cooperating with the security people marking and following the criminals. He reminded the chief that they could continue their duties because of the residents' cooperation. He gave an example of a criminal armed with a panga against security men in Nemburi sub-location at night, and the residents came out with pangas, rungus, and other arms and weapons. In good number, he surrendered before any physical confrontations that could have led to death, maiming him, or making an arrest.

"In other cases, residents make the arrest and call us to collect the alleged criminal, and our work becomes easier and more convenient." The chairman said that was the best way possible to work together.

www.ingramcontent.com/pod-product-compliance
Ingram Content Group UK Ltd.
Pitfield, Milton Keynes, MK11 3LW, UK
UKHW041348190726
13845UKWH00026B/484

9 789393 734099